MO

AMBITION DOESN'T WAIT FOR LADY FORTUNE

Yuriy Novodvorski

First published in paperback by
Michael Terence Publishing in 2025
www.mtp.agency

Copyright © 2025 Yuriy Novodvorski

Yuriy Novodvorski has asserted the right to be identified as
the author of this work in accordance with the
Copyright, Designs and Patents Act 1988

ISBN 9781800949652

This is a work of fiction. Any names or characters,
businesses or places, events or incidents, are fictitious.
Any resemblance to actual persons, living or dead,
or actual events is purely coincidental

No part of this publication may be reproduced, stored
in a retrieval system, or transmitted, in any form or
by any means, electronic, mechanical, photocopying,
recording or otherwise, without the prior
permission of the publisher

Cover design (AI)
by Michael Terence Publishing

Translated from Ukrainian
by Olga Loza

Illustrations
by Anna Kopyl

Edited
by Sam Harvey

Foreword 5

Intro.
What came first 7

Part 1.
Kyiv 35

Part 2.
Reykjavík: The secret of the Atlantic 141

Part 3.
Roman holiday 209

Foreword

It was said in ancient Rome that every person is the architect of their own fortune. Your actions and your thoughts, your self-confidence, your circumstances, and countless other factors decide whether the infamous and universally beloved, the mysterious and fickle, Lady Fortune will pay her heed to you. Maybe sometimes it seems that she's all but forgotten about you, but isn't it just like her to appear when you least expect it. She's fickle like that, and it's true that she doesn't possess the most even temper. But once her attention falls on you, your world will turn upside down. Everything will change. And not everyone can cope with the twists and turns that will follow…

Intro.

What came first

After what happened in 2014 – after all those people across Ukraine rose up in the Revolution of Dignity, offering their lives as payment for the brighter, fairer future they so longed for – everyone's eyes shone with hope. A hope for change, for a fair and honest government that would imprison all the corrupt officials and thugs. A government that would take care of the country. Then, in the blink of an eye, Russia annexed Crimea as the Ukrainian government helplessly watched on. Russian troops entered and captured Crimea almost without resistance. Locals were fooled by promises of "mountains of gold" – and with that, having therefore "secured" the "support" of people in Crimea, Russia held a referendum. Those same citizens were asked, at gunpoint, whether they wanted to join Russia. Whether they wanted it to be "official." And that wasn't even the last of it. The Kremlin decided that Crimea wasn't enough and deployed troops in the east of Ukraine. In response, Ukraine launched the Anti-Terrorist Operation, what we call the ATO. The operation should have lasted just days, or at most weeks, but it stretched into years. The war in Donbas claimed thousands of lives, made thousands of orphans, and left in its wake who knows how many disfigured bodies and souls.

Most people across Ukraine are of modest means – which is to say that they balance precariously on the verge of poverty. Many are capable of desperate and reckless things – which might be to say that they all want to live. And by live you might mostly mean survive. Think back on that one Tupac Shakur line: "Only God can judge me."

Sometime in the mid-90s, Danylo Dumanskyi was born in Ivano-Frankivsk in western Ukraine. His family never had much money while he was growing up, but life taught him to find joy in small things and appreciate honest people. From a young age, he had to learn to trust his intuition, to rely only on himself, and to be able to make – and take responsibility for – his own decisions. Danylo didn't do particularly well in school, but he did have one invaluable skill: he knew how to make something out of nothing. Without making any particular effort to study, Danylo made the grades he needed thanks to his keen eye, wit, and ingenuity. This seemed to suit everyone. He had a big family: he had his mom, his dad, his older sister Veronika, and his younger brother Mykhailo. When Danylo was in high school, the family's financial situation improved significantly. His mom, Olena, an experienced otolaryngologist, started making more money when she got a job at a private clinic, while his dad, Andrii Yaroslavovych, started his own business – something to do with car parts – that did pretty well. After graduating high school, Danylo had to choose a university. At that time, what university a kid would attend was more often than not decided by their parents. Their lack of agency in that decision and widespread corruption in universities meant that a degree hardly offered kids a key to a happy and successful future. Unless, of course, the family also took that extra step, smoothing their progeny's academic progress by bribing university staff. But not all parents had the means – or the connections – to do so, or to be able to secure a post-university job for their kid. Danylo's mom and dad, given their combined years of experience, believed that they knew best what their son should do. They convinced him that his best option was to enter the Lviv National University, Faculty of Economics. Andrii Yaroslavovych was particularly insistent on the field. Olena mentioned a medical degree a few times, but gave up when she realized that Danylo didn't care much about medicine. Besides, his older sister Veronika had only a couple months of residency left and would be a doctor soon.

Lviv welcomed Danylo with open arms. Nightclubs, drunken parties that lasted into the early hours of the morning, missed classes, a constant lack of money, and the eternal apathy that you could say was characteristic of students then.

Danylo had liked music since he was a kid, and he gradually gained recognition as a DJ – first among friends, then among wider audiences. He had perfect pitch and a good sense of rhythm. DJing opened things up for him: new friendships, popularity, and financial stability – it paid well. Thankfully, he had a good head on his shoulders, as the saying goes: he knew when to stop and didn't play in clubs that much, only twice a week – once during the work week, and once on the weekend – so his studies weren't too affected.

After a year of getting to know Lviv and the kids who lived there, Danylo and two friends-and-also-flatmates came up with a business idea. They bought weed in Ivano-Frankivsk and sold it in Lviv. They sold weed in good, large quantities, without petty haggling, which minimized the risks. They had no trouble finding customers. Sometimes – because of his DJ work, because of his friendliness and sociability – Danylo felt like he knew half the city.

People smoked weed across the world. Cannabis has medicinal properties. It'd been legalized in some US states and in Canada – so why couldn't it be legalized in post-Soviet countries? Because it's better to have a population hooked on booze, so that they think less, and their lives deteriorate at a faster rate? Low-quality alcohol is practically a chemical weapon. But people were afraid to talk about it openly.

To the friends, the business idea seemed flawless. They gave thought to its most minute details. They brought the weed to Lviv twice a month, agreeing that each of them would take turns arranging its transportation. Since none of them had a car, they relied on their parents – their unsuspecting dads, to be precise – who would never have guessed that every couple of weeks their cars were being used to transport the finest Carpathian weed. *So what?* they thought. *We're just trying to get by.* Danylo met Tolik, a rich Roma (Gypsy) kid dating his classmate. Tolik told his friends, and like that business kept getting better and better. The business went strong for a couple of months, until who but Lady Fortuna showed up and forced them to shutter it.

On a sunny Monday, the parents of one of Danylo's flatmates, Ruslan, came to Lviv on personal business. While in town, they thought they'd also visit Ruslan, to pick up some Tupperware they used to send food to their son and his flatmates, and to meet the flat's owner to discuss the rent. No notice of course, so while Ruslan and his flatmates dozed off at their lectures, their business dealings were being, unbeknownst to them, exposed. Ruslan's parents and the owner of the flat, Svitlana Heorhiivna, arrived at the apartment, and after Ruslan's mom picked up her Tupperware, she decided to have a quick look inside his wardrobe, just to see if everything in there was folded away neat and tidy. And what did she find but a bag with more than two kilos of weed and around 100 grams of finest-quality cannabis buds? Instead of putting it back where she found it and asking her son about the bag's contents, she – a naïve and curious woman – brought the bag out into the kitchen and asked her husband, in full view of owner Svitlana Heorhiivna:

"What are these herbs I found in Ruslan's things?"

There was a tense moment of silence before Ruslan's dad and Svitlana Heorhiivna realized what was in the bag. As it dawned on them, events began to unfold with the intensity of a Bollywood action movie. Svitlana Heorhiivna – a prudish woman with a penchant for snitching, shaped by her Soviet upbringing – wouldn't hear another word from Ruslan's parents. As she called the police, yelling into the receiver that her property has been turned into a drug den, neighbors came running to see what all the commotion was about. Ruslan's parents just stood there, dazed and in the middle of a dream they'd never dreamt. The cops arrived some twenty minutes later as neighbors crowded the hallway. Ruslan's mom called an ambulance, fearing that she was about to have a heart attack, while his dad – hair going gray, pale as a corpse – hustled on the phone to bury the incident, calling everyone he knew who could help. He rushed from his wife's side to Svitlana Heorhiivna and from Svitlana Heorhiivna to the policeman, who, impervious to the chaos around him, filled in his incident report.

In a few days everything had evened out, thanks to Ukraine's infamous corruption. A bribe here, a bribe there, and lo and behold, the dust had settled, all was clear. But while the cops and the flat owner were relatively easy to appease – the guys got off cheap, in fact – and Danylo and his friends managed to hold on to their spots at the university, they still got a good bashing from their parents. They would no longer live together, their parents decided, and from then on, they did what they could to limit how much the friends saw each other. And while there's no point going into the specifics of the punishment each of the three received, each of their lives changed after that day. Neither of the guys were particularly sorry about what they'd done, but they learned a valuable lesson: they would each be more cautious and circumspect in their business affairs.

Ruslan, who seemed to take the incident to heart more than the other two, threw himself into his studies. His concern with his parents' opinion of him drove him to do everything he could to get on their good side. He passed all his exams with flying colors, working hard to secure a reputation as a promising young lawyer. Vadym, the third flatmate, decided to stay with his relatives in the US, giving up on his university degree in Ukraine. Out of the three of them, Vadym was the most average, boring person; there was nothing particularly worth knowing about him. Danylo, meanwhile, continued his studies, though with mixed success. But he came into his own in Lviv. He kept DJing and was fairly successful. About a year after the incident at the flat, Danylo fell in love for the first time. Young people from all over Ukraine – and beyond – were coming to study in Lviv, and someone as young, handsome, and friendly as Danylo had no trouble on the love front. He had always been popular with girls; he liked having friends with benefits and enjoyed affairs. His casual relationships often culminated in hot, sex-filled weekends. That was all the norm for him. All sorts of women had woken up in his apartment at one point or another: students, models, daughters of politicians and prosecutors, singers, waitresses, and even his university lecturers. Don Juan would have been jealous.

But love struck him when he least expected it. As it goes. Danylo was ordering a vodka - Red Bull after playing a set at the Pozitiff club. It was Students' Day and lots of first-year students were out. The crowd at the bar made it nearly impossible to get the bartenders' attention. But Danylo, who knew everyone working at the club, ordered what he wanted with ease. While he stood by the bar with his friends, he felt someone tap him on his shoulder. He thought it must be a friend, but when he turned around, he saw a petite girl with brown eyes, beautiful long black hair, and a disarming smile. Danylo froze. He felt as though time had stopped, as if the press of the crowd around them melted away. It was just the two of them there.

"I'm sorry," the girl said, "could you get some water for me? It's impossible to get anyone's attention. Here's the money, I'd be so grateful."

Danylo felt as though he'd entered a different dimension. Everything around him lost focus and he could barely speak.

"Okay," he managed.

And that was the beginning of their love story. Diana also studied at the Lviv National University but majored in journalism. She was from Chernivtsi, a city some 130 kilometers away from Danylo's native Ivano-Frankivsk. It seemed that their meeting was fated. It felt like they were made for each other, and they knew it. They spent almost every moment of the following few months together. Love changed Danylo; it gave him a new wind. From a perpetually sleep-deprived and bored student, he became a happy and cheerful young man. His university grades improved too. And Diana changed, blossoming into young womanhood. Danylo gave her all of his love and attention, which in turn gave her confidence and made her feel loved and wanted. Her heart and soul were warmed on the flame of his care and attention. Their mutual attraction was undeniable, peaking during a trip to Prague on New Year's Eve. Their love grew stronger and stronger.

One day in winter, Danylo woke up to a phone call. It was his mom. She told him that earlier that morning, his dad had been in a car accident and was now in intensive care. His condition was severe. She sounded worried. With his firm underperforming, Andrii

Yaroslavovych had started drinking more. He was driving after a long evening of drinking with friends – something that happened more and more now – and had lost control of his car, crashing into a truck at high speed.

Wasting no time, Danylo packed his bag and took the first bus to Ivano-Frankivsk. That evening, his father's heart stopped beating. His death turned the lives of many people upside down. After he was buried, the Dumanskyi family faced many trials, and their quiet and comfortable life turned into a tangle of problems, which fell on the shoulders of Andrii Yaroslavovych's widow, Olena, and his eldest son Danylo.

In an effort to save his firm, Danylo's dad had borrowed money from people who were dangerous just to know, let alone be used as lenders. No one other than those thugs knew how much money Andrii Yaroslavovych owed, so naturally, the amount was exaggerated.

Danylo and his mom sold everything there was to sell to repay the debt. Miraculously, they managed to hold on to the family home and the small summer house in the mountains, which no one other than the family knew about. But all this meant that Danylo couldn't keep studying full-time; over the next exam period, he transferred to a part-time program. His relationship with Diana was deteriorating. He no longer had time to give her the attention she was used to, and she struggled to adjust to the new reality – one in which she wasn't the center of his universe. Danylo was forced out of his romantic and carefree student existence to the bitter and unpredictable reality of being an adult. Maybe all Diana had to do was exercise some patience and let the extreme emotions of those first few weeks after Danylo's father's death subside, but she did the opposite, convincing herself that he didn't need her anymore. She decided that she was free to explore her other options and find a new boyfriend. Diana was a striking, charismatic young woman – it didn't take much to find herself at the center of male attention. She knew how to get someone to fall for her, and she enjoyed her power. And so Artem Markov appeared on her horizon – whether that was written in the stars or just a small coincidence. Artem, who was also studying at the Lviv National University to be a lawyer, was the son of a well-known Lviv business owner and the future heir to his dad's company. Little did Diana know that he was also a future pain in his dad's ass who'd have to be sent to Israel, or elsewhere, to have his septum replaced for his love of sniffing cocaine. Of course, she had no idea of the scale of Artem's addiction. For her, he was a handsome and stylish young man, dressed head to toe in luxury Italian brands and with a new Lexus to boot. His glitz and glamour were undeniably enticing. And although Diana was never particularly calculating and never seemed to chase money, this time she fell for it. At first, they hung out with mutual friends, and soon enough Artem was offering her lifts home. We all know how that ends. Danylo, meanwhile, had stayed in touch with friends in Lviv, and heard what was happening through them. Here and there he worried but didn't give it much thought. Dealing with his family's affairs relieved his focus from the possibility that some rich kid was flirting with his girlfriend. Danylo was certain that his relationship with Diana was grounded in sincere mutual feelings. And besides, he didn't take guys like Artem seriously. Not that he despised them – he knew and was friendly with many of them – but they were never close friends.

By spring, the Dumanskyi family's financial affairs deteriorated further. Danylo got a job as a sales representative. He was good at it, but despite doing his best to succeed didn't see many prospects in that line of work. His relationship with Diana ended abruptly, in a way he didn't expect. She wouldn't pick up his calls, and then Danylo would find out from mutual friends that she was out clubbing with her new friends. Without fighting or drama, they stopped talking to each other. It was almost instantaneous, as if there had never been anything between them. Life is often like that, testing the people around you: some of them turn out to be snakes whose hissing you mistakenly take for heavenly singing, while others turn out to be wolves prepared to stand by you until your last breath. Well, that might be a bit much, but something like that…

His father's death made Danylo appreciate the true value of money: It disappeared from his pockets He realized how difficult it is to make it and how easily it's spent. He was used to a comfortable life of not necessarily spending money on a whim, being able to afford nice things. He found the change difficult, and it made him unhappy.

After he graduated, Danylo spent a few years working in sales before going back to his previous line of work: Weed. This time though, he took it much more seriously. The scale of the operation was much larger. One Friday night Danylo met up with his childhood friends Ivan Tatarchuk and Maksym Kurzaiev. They hadn't seen each other in a while. Max lived in Kyiv and didn't visit much, and Ivan had recently had a son. Both struggled to find time to meet up with friends. Each found family, work, and routine so consuming that they could only dream about cold beers with the guys. After a few pints, Danylo, Ivan, and Max were waxing nostalgic about the past and somehow got to talking about how Danylo and his two friends had dealt weed in Lviv before being busted, thanks to a stupid coincidence. The discussion turned to how things could have gone had circumstances been different. They talked through imaginary scenarios, laughing, and the conversation turned to the present. They talked about corruption and lawlessness in Ukraine, about wanting better lives, and the desire to make more money.

"Why not take another chance," Ivan asked, "and get involved with good old weed again? But this time, we do it more diligently, more meticulously."

Max and Danylo's eyes shone. Hungry for extra income, the three met again over coffee the next day, and each brought to the table ideas on how to bring the plan to life. Max was supposed to travel back to Kyiv that evening, so the conversation felt urgent.

The plan went like this: Each of the three would have different responsibilities. Max would oversee sales in

Kyiv. He knew lots of people there, and many already engaged in illicit business. He knew real gangsters with connections all over Ukraine, from Luhansk in the east to Lviv in the west. Ivan – head of the Ivano-Frankivsk branch of Future Post, Ukraine's largest delivery firm – would be in charge of logistics. Ivan, in other words, would get the weed from Point A to Point B. He had long-haul drivers he trusted and was able to easily settle matters with Future Post's internal security service to ensure the smooth and reliable transit of goods. Danylo was tasked with growing top-quality weed – perhaps the most difficult mission. He turned the small plot of land that his family's summer house stood on into a state-of-the-art marijuana farm. Grandpa Mykola, a family friend, had been looking after the land and the house for many years: one of the first tasks Danylo faced was convincing him of the worth and necessity of shifting the farm's focus. Despite his old age, Mykola was fairly progressive; he also knew what Danylo had been through. Mykola respected Danylo's father and treated Danylo as his own grandson – so despite the risks involved, he agreed without much pushback to help in every way he could. A huge advantage of the house was that it was connected to the electricity mains, which made it possible to grow weed there year-round. Within a matter of days, Ivan, Max, and Danylo bought all the necessary equipment: grow boxes and tents, sodium lamps and LED-lights, and electromagnetic regulators that automatically ensured smooth heating of the lamps and protected the equipment from power surges. They bought extractor fans and ventilators to ensure good air circulation and prevent the smell from accumulating in the building, and installed an irrigation system, as well as timers and climate control sensors to ensure the plants would receive enough light and to minimize human labor. Their entire underground operation was headquartered at the farm, which sat near the village of Snidavka in the Kosiv district of Ivano-Frankivsk. An idyllic wooden house; a roof among enchanting woods and meadows, hidden away from tourists' curious eyes among the trees and behind a fence. There was a well in the yard, a grill, and a small outbuilding. The house's fairly new windows overlooked the Carpathians, impossibly beautiful. The Ternoshory tract, with its mysterious rocky formations among pines and spruce trees, was just a few miles away. Danylo's dad had loved the house and tried to invest in renovations whenever he had money to spare. The Dumanskyi family had visited frequently through Danylo's childhood, and the house held a special place in his heart. When he thought of the house, memories of cooking dinner with his parents, rock-climbing, and playing hide-and-seek with his siblings flooded his head.

Grandpa Mykola was well-known and respected in those parts. Danylo's dad Andrii Yaroslavovych had always helped he and his family with money. The locals, knowing that Mykola looked after the house, didn't dare enter the plot. They wouldn't damage the land or steal anything from the property – out of respect for Mykola. He was a wise and cunning man. Locals often deferred to his opinion and many of them may have feared him. He had strong arms, and more than one person had his teeth kicked in by Mykola. He had no shortage of lady friends either, and his love affairs were the stuff of legend. He ate honey, nuts, and a tincture made from the yellow gentian root. His health in his older years was example for all the local youths.

After all the equipment was installed and Danylo and his friends showed Grandpa Mykola how everything worked, he invited them to his table, on which sat a bottle of homemade honey mead, a piece of cured *salo,* and a hunk of fresh sheep's cheese, *brynza.* It had been a stressful day, and Ivan and Danylo were glad for the offerings. They wanted to relax.

There aren't many jobs in Ukrainian villages for young people. Lots leave to work abroad in Poland, Slovakia and Czechia. Danylo and his friends suggested that Mykola find a few young guys he could trust to help him – there was more work than one person could comfortably do, especially because they hoped to grow weed not just on Danylo's family's plot of land, but also in the nearby woods. They'd scouted out a few suitable locations. A couple of handy youths could also help Mykola figure out all the equipment he would have to operate to grow the weed indoors, in the house.

Grandpa Mykola poured each of them some mead, scratched his head, thought for a few seconds, and told the guys that he had a couple people in mind. Then Mykola got up from the table, rushing away and saying that in a couple hours he'd bring his potential helpers over. The guys loved Mykola's proactive approach. Two hours later, he returned with three teenage boys in tow. While Danylo set the table and Ivan finished up the grilling, Mykola vouched for the three boys, saying they could absolutely be trusted. It was enough for Danylo: he took Grandpa Mykola at his word. The man never promised anything he couldn't deliver. Two of the boys, Taras and Vitalik Humeniuk, were brothers. Their dad had gone to Russia ten years ago and was never heard from again. No one knows what happened to him. Their mother had died from a serious illness five years ago, and they lived with their grandparents. Taras, the younger, was soon to start his last year of high school, while his elder brother Vitalik had spent the last two years trying to dodge compulsory military service. He couldn't – and didn't really want to – go to university, so he worked temporary jobs and helped his family around the house. The third boy, Vasia, went by the nickname *"Pes"* (Dog), because he had always dressed in old, torn rags when he was little. Vasia came from a troubled family. His parents didn't care for him, choosing to drink instead. Grandpa Mykola, his neighbor, had practically raised him. Vasia had just graduated from high school and didn't want to study anymore. These three boys – Taras, Vitalik and Vasia – had nothing to lose. They saw Mykola's offer as an opportunity to make money and leave their circumstances behind. they were all smart, resourceful and hard-working, good listeners, and eager to learn. But most importantly, they knew how to keep their mouths shut and respected their elders. The deal was sealed.

From that moment on, time flew by. The team worked well together and already it was time to harvest the first crop, which turned out much better – in terms of both quality and quantity – than any of them had hoped. Danylo and his partners were over the moon: their idea worked, and ahead of them lay a bright future.

This excellent weed was transported from the small plot in the village of Snidavka to Ivano-Frankivsk, usually in the middle of the night, to avoid unnecessary attention. Vitalik and Vasia packed the weed into hermetically sealed bags, which they then put into a large duffel stuffed with dried porcini – to conceal the bag's true cargo. The pungent dried mushrooms also obscured the smell of the weed. Danylo and Ivan brought bags of weed and mushrooms to the Future Post branch in Ivano-Frankivsk, where it was picked up by drivers in on the deal and who brought it to Kyiv, where Max sold it to local hucksters, who were always keen for more luxury Carpathian weed.

The arrangement worked successfully for months. There was demand for weed in the big city, but the amount of weed Danylo and his friends were bringing in was not large enough to be to the detriment of someone else's business; besides, Max had connections in those circles. The Carpathian weed – or *Karpatka*, as it was called in Kyiv – wasn't giving anyone headaches. All the while, Danylo and his friends gained more and more prominence. They became known to people with power and sway, and people who knew Danylo and his friends respected them.

This kind of attention couldn't go unnoticed higher up. Anatolii Levchenko – businessman and politician, member of the Verkhovna Rada (Ukrainian Parliament) and the co-owner of one of the largest Ukrainian banks, a hotel chain, and a number of other businesses of various degrees of legality – has trained a keen eye on what the three friends were doing. Levchenko, just back from Cancun, Mexico, where he often travelled on business and holidays with his girlfriend, was in dire need of people for his new business venture. He had just been given a green light to import cocaine to Kyiv. He wasn't the sole proprietor of the business, or the only person involved in its management – there were bigger fish in that particular pond – but he was given a share, and, importantly, protection. As always, any kind of agreement in that line of work was rather fragile, and while the ice they walked on was thin, more often than not the possibility of windfall profits offset the fear, the worry, the anxiety they had. The thirst for profit was powerful.

It worked like this: the cocaine would arrive to the port of Constanța in Romania. Constanța served smugglers as a window to Europe through which any amount of just about anything could be smuggled. As long as those using it were generous in their gratitude. Why not the port of Odesa in southern Ukraine? Political instability was generally the answer; the government could change at any moment, and business dealings would be ratted out to the police and the special services. The Odesa port just wasn't reliable enough. Too many vultures circled it. The port of Constanța was entirely different: cocaine from Latin

America had been imported there for decades, and Romanians had earned a reputation as top-notch professionals in the smuggling business. Corruption in Romania was widespread as ever, and locals enjoyed their expensive cars and beautiful lovers, and so never said no to a good deal.

And perhaps most importantly, they knew not to mess around with Ukrainians. A deal with a Ukrainian was always upheld.

Through intermediaries, Levchenko got in touch with Danylo and arranged to meet him in Kyiv. There was no time to waste: the first batch of cocaine was due to arrive to Constanța the next month, Levchenko needed people. Ivan and Danylo travelled to Kyiv the day after the call and crashed at Max's. Realizing the magnitude of their situation, the friends refrained from discussing where the meeting with Levchenko could lead. Their approach was: whatever happens, happens. They knew they couldn't have said no to someone like Levchenko.

The group met at one of the trendy hotels Levchenko owned. Levchenko was represented by Kostia Khriashch (Gristle), the businessman's left-hand man, his most trusted associate. Kostia told them everything they needed to know.

"Kostia, we'll do a beautiful job," Danylo said.

After talking with Kostia, they were joined by Levchenko, who was eager to meet them. In his mind, he saw the three friends as Desperados.

Once back in Ivano-Frankivsk, Danylo wasted no time. He had to find a place to rent in the Verkhovyna district, up in the mountains and close to the Ukrainian border with Romania, somewhere away from curious eyes. He also needed people who would work for him. Neither the Humeniuk brothers nor Vasia "Pes" seemed to be the right people for the job. They were still kids, and a lot of money was at stake. After consulting with Ivan, Danylo decided to ask an old friend of his, Sasha Tarnavskyi.

Sasha was a former athlete, a successful boxer. He owned a security firm. Danylo had known him for a long time, and the two had been through lots together. Sasha was streetwise and knew how to avoid trouble. When they were younger, Danylo and Sasha had stood together whenever they'd found themselves in the middle of a fight. Sasha loved – no, worshipped – money. As soon as he heard Danylo's offer, he was all in. He recommended trustworthy people; employment in Ukraine was lagging and Sasha knew none of them would turn down Danylo's lucrative offer. The offer easily topped the average salary in the region. Levchenko gave Danylo and his friends around $80,000 to organize everything. They bought two off-road vehicles and a quadcopter for reconnaissance operations; they rented a house in the mountains and made purchases to make it more livable. The guys who were to live in the mountain house had a simple task: they'd spend two weeks at a time there, waiting for a phone call or text message with coordinates of the location where they would pick up the coke. Up in the mountains, the border between Romania and Ukraine is porous and barely protected – a smuggler's dream. At first, four guys stayed at the house together, waiting to be given the pick-up location. They later agreed two would be enough. The elder Humeniuk brother or Vasia Pes would sometimes come help them. The guys had two-week shifts, and the team's plan seemed to work without a hitch: traffic between Constanța–Verkhovyna–Ivano-Frankivsk–Kyiv ran smoothly. Sasha and Danylo enforced strict discipline on everyone involved. People causing trouble were replaced and punished early on, and everyone who remained treated their work seriously and earnestly.

Levchenko was pleased with how his squad of Desperados organized everything. The new venture was bringing neat sums of cash into his coffers. Once it was obvious that Danylo and his friends would carry out what was asked of them, Levchenko decided to involve himself in another sensitive affair. With parliamentary elections coming up, Levchenko was desperate to hold on to his seat. To lose his seat would be to lose his prestige, his status, his parliamentary immunity, and all the other privileges that came along with it. Winning the elections was, to be put simply, a matter of absolute necessity.

Levchenko sent Kostia and his squad to Ivano-Frankivsk to convince Danylo and co. to put together a group of people who would collect information on Levchenko's political rivals. Levchenko wanted dirt. Being an opposition candidate made what Levchenko was asking even riskier, but he knew that Danylo and his friends had no option other than succumb to his request.

Levchenko rented a luxury villa near the village of Mykulychyn in the Carpathians for Kostia's meeting with Danylo. As soon as Kostia arrived, he gathered everyone at a table and relayed Levchenko's request. Danylo, Ivan, and Sasha fell silent. They didn't speak. Each somewhat in shock, each seeing that things were getting serious – too serious for a rash response. The guys needed to take a time-out and to work it out among themselves first. Danylo asked Kostia for a day to digest the information and give him an answer. Kostia agreed; he was fine with that.

During the party that followed, not all the attendees were in the mood for fun. After the arrivals from Kyiv had their fair share of whiskey and cocaine and retreated to their rooms with the strippers brought in for the occasion, Danylo and his two friends finally sat down to discuss their course of action. They didn't have much time to make a decision, and the stakes were high. They were doubly high for Ivan and Sasha, both of whom were married and had kids. They both understood the danger Levchenko's offer entailed. It was one thing to run their business back home, where everyone knew everyone, and it was relatively easy to settle any issues or emergencies that might crop. Moving to Kyiv, one of the most dangerous cities in Europe, involved a totally different set of risks and considerations. Even the most minor slip-up could get you killed, by foe – or friend. Danylo's situation was different: he wasn't in a relationship and starting a family wasn't really on his horizon. He focused on work instead. Subconsciously, he'd known as soon as he heard Kostia's proposal that he would say yes. The way Kostia explained it, the group that would be put together to gather dirt about Levchenko's opponents was only going to exist until the elections.

After hours of discussion, Danylo, Sasha, and Ivan decided that only the former two would go to Kyiv – along with a couple other trustworthy guys, while Ivan would stay in the west to oversee their cocaine operations. They worked out the kinks in their trafficking system. They'd start using a garbage truck to get the cocaine from the Carpathians to Ivano-Frankivsk. It was easy to bribe a driver, and besides no one would want to stop and search a garbage truck in the middle of the night.

During breakfast the next morning, Danylo told Kostia that they made up their minds and were ready to take on their new task.

Part 1.

Kyiv

Sasha and Danylo arrived in Kyiv on a Friday night, hoping to acclimatize to big city life over the weekend. Levchenko expected their arrival. He rented an apartment in Pechersk, practically in the heart of Kyiv, for Sasha and Danylo. The flat was in a luxury newbuild and had two bedrooms, a living room, two bathrooms, and a kitchen. It would be difficult to find more comfortable accommodation. The Desperados squad was also given three cars: a Volkswagen T5, a Toyota Land Cruiser, and a Skoda Octavia. The squad – besides Danylo and Sasha – included another five members, hand-picked by Danylo, who knew that failure was not an option and that they had to fulfil Levchenko's brief under any circumstances. Those five lived separately on the left bank of the river Dnipro, near the Pozniaky metro station.

At nine on Monday morning, Danylo and Sasha set out to pick up the bugs, wires, and weapons they needed for their spying operation. As they got out of their black VW T5 in an industrial neighborhood on the outskirts of Kyiv, a silver Range Rover with blacked out windows parked nearby, and a balding 40-year-old man stepped out.

"Hey guys," he yelled, "I got the goods!"

So they met Mishania another serious black market player and a good friend of Kostia Khriashch.

"Hello, hello! Show us what you got," Danylo fired back.

"Look: ten wires, five smoke detectors with built-in cameras, three wall clocks with built-in WiFi-enabled cameras, a fucking incredible jammer to suppress mobile and internet communication signals, a field indicator for detecting bugs and hidden cameras, and – look at this scanner!" He pointed at a code grabber for opening and closing cars, "It's one of the newest models. It'll set Levchenko back $4,000, but that's hardly anything for him. There's also eight sets of walkie-talkies and matching headsets, a video camera with a powerful zoom, binoculars, and a monocular. The guns are coming in tomorrow, the guys are bringing them from Kharkiv. There are no bump stocks on them, so don't be alarmed. I think that's it. You can reach me through Kostia," he wrapped up. "Good luck and see you soon."

"Thanks for now, Mishania," Danylo said, pressing a foil-wrapped package of top-notch cocaine into Mishania's hand, "Be well. This is a present from us."

Mishania drove away, and so did Danylo and Sasha, the two glad that the rendezvous had gone well. With the pick-up officially launching their operation, they began preparations. That evening, there was an all-hands-on-deck meeting with the rest of the Desperados squad. Kostia was scheduled to come and give them the rundown on the challengers of Levchenko that they were supposed to collect dirt on.

Danylo and the six other Desperados members arrived at the address provided by Kostia in the town of Kotsiubynske, just outside of Kyiv, at 7pm sharp. The large house was set in the woods just back from a scenic lake, all belonging to Levchenko, who had decided to temporarily lend it over to the Desperados squad as their headquarters. As soon as Danylo's VW T5 approached the gates, they opened. Danylo and his squad, and Kostia and two of his acolytes settled into an enormous living room decorated like a hunting lodge. With everyone on edge, Kostia began.

"Guys, I don't think I need to say again how important this is to Levchenko. You all know it, so I'll get down to business. At this point, Levchenko has two main opponents in this race: Hennadi Trofimov, an old-school, Russian-leaning politician backed by the Kremlin who has been in politics for decades and has held various top positions in government agencies. He's been the deputy Minister of Infrastructure of Ukraine for the past couple of years. Now he suddenly really wants to get elected to parliament, likely on Moscow's orders. As far as I know, he has two security guards constantly at his side; they're both former KGB operatives and come with all the baggage that implies. We need as much information as possible about Trofimov. My guys have been trailing his every movement for the past three months, so I can give you his detailed schedule. We have information about his wife and children, and his little vices. I hope all this will help you do your job."

Kostia poured himself a glass of orange juice. "Do you have any questions?" he asked.

Sasha raised his hand. "Kostia, I have an idea. Why don't we trap Trofimov – or his wife or son? We can manipulate them until we get the dirt we need. Given how much we know about their weaknesses, I don't think it'd be impossible. What do you think?" Sasha asked Kostia, looking him right in the eye.

The room grew tense, and the tension hung there. Finally, Kostia smirked.

"I'm all for it. And I think Levchenko will be too. But the question is," he asked slowly, "do you have the guts to carry it out? No offence, but it won't be quite as easy as you might think."

"We have guts alright, we'll manage," Danylo said, exchanging a glance with Sasha.

"Well, then you've got a go-ahead from me. I'll send you all the information we've got so far tomorrow. You can start hustling," Kostia said, before continuing on to Levchenko's second opponent.

"Stanislav Panchyshyn is also dreaming of a seat in the parliament. He's a nationalist and a persuasive public speaker. He's also volunteering to help the guys fighting on the front, or at least that's the image he's cultivating on social media. In reality, he's just a scammer. He may be hanging around people who really do help our guys on the front line, but it's all for show, to create an image. We've also been working on him. We bugged his house and have been listening in for a while. He and his buddies set up a couple of charities that they use for money-laundering. He's a heavy drinker and fentanyl user. Divorced his wife last year. He's in the *Sovist Narodu* (People's Conscience) party, close with party leaders. He's young, unscrupulous, and ambitious, People's Conscience are betting on him to take our constituency. It'll be even easier to get dirt on him than on Trofimov, but be careful," Kostia said.

He discussed a few more things with Danylo and Sasha, made a plan for the next day, and wrapped up the meeting. Everyone left. They were all prepared to do their best and achieve the results that were expected of them. When they got to their flat, Danylo asked if Sasha wanted to go out for dinner to talk through everything that happened that day. Sasha was glad to be asked. He'd been starving for the past three hours and could've put down a large steak or a pizza, with extra cheese of course. There was a tiny Italian restaurant just outside their building – an obvious choice for their dinner.

As they sat down, Danylo looked at Sasha, "Do you think we'll manage? What's your gut feeling? Be honest. But between the two of us," he said. "Don't get all philosophical and beat around the bush."

"As far as I'm concerned, the three candidates have about the same chances of winning before all these election battles. Levchenko might have a bit of an advantage, which we should use. My gut's telling me we're in for a wild ride. What do you think?" Sasha smiled wryly and went back to his menu.

"I think when it comes to Trofimov, we should start with his family, not him personally," Danylo said. "I think it'll be easier to find a weak point there. I can't figure Panchyshyn out though. It all seems too easy, which is making me worry. On the one hand, all of his shortcomings are in plain view, and it should be easy to use them to our advantage, but on the other hand, he's a public figure, and he's all over social media. And a volunteer! Any dirt about him might be interpreted – or misinterpreted – as efforts by the Kremlin to disqualify a pro-Ukrainian candidate. Panchyshyn will just present himself as an innocent victim. Something's telling me that People's Conscience might be prepared for something like that to happen. But anyway, Panchyshyn has his own skeletons in the closet, which he's going to real lengths to hide. I think he's highly controlling how much of himself he reveals to his opponents. I'm sure he knows he's being watched. He's shrewd like a rat." Danylo sat back.

"Let's park this conversation for a second and order. I feel like my head's about to explode from all this Game of Thrones bullshit."

"Sounds good to me," Danylo said, hearing Kostia's hungry plea. "Let's order. Haven't eaten since the morning. Time for a big meal."

Each tired but smiling, the two friends set aside the work chat, called over a waiter, ordered, and – trying to carry themselves even further away from work concerns – talked about the Dynamo Kyiv and Shakhtar Donetsk football game the day before.

By the end of that week, the Desperados were all in on the brief. Danylo and Sasha carefully went through all the information that Kostia had given them and relayed everything to the rest of their squad. Panchyshyn and Trofimov would be observed for three days. The Desperados also started watching Trofimov's family. It was the family who Danylo and co. would use to discredit and blackmail Trofimov, the pro-Russian cunt. The group also found potential leads on Panchyshyn. They dug deeper. The guys at the Kotsiubynske base stayed up late into the night analyzing the information obtained in Kyiv.

Early one morning, around 7:15am, Danylo and two squad members, Hrisha and Serhii parked their inconspicuous navy-blue Skoda Octavia on Yurii Illienko Street, not far from the Institute of International Relations of the Taras Shevchenko National University. They were waiting for Yelyzaveta, or Liza, Trofimova, Trofimov's daughter, to show up at university. Their goal was to wiretap her car while she was in class. They didn't expect it to be difficult as Liza emphatically refused security and always drove the car herself. She missed her first scheduled class, but Danylo and the guys kept waiting.

"This Liza isn't bad," Danylo said, looking at her photos on Facebook.

"Looks like she's smart, too. Doesn't have too much stuff online – almost everyone else in her position would've posted a lot more. She only has three photos," Serhii said, looking over Danylo's shoulder.

"As far as I know, she's supposed to do an internship soon as part of her studies. We need to find out where she's going to intern and when. That's urgent."

They remained in the car for another hour, beginning to think that they'd have to leave empty-handed when things started to happen.

"Look, here comes our princess!" Hrisha said, pointing at Trofimova's car.

A new, white Porsche Macan parked nearby. A young, blonde woman got out of the car. She had an athletic build and plump, gently-Botoxed lips. She was dressed in a sharp suit with an Yves Saint Laurent coat and carried an Hermès bag. She wore Chanel sunglasses from the latest collection and her golden hair was pulled back into a neat ponytail. She looked spectacular. As she walked down the street, men turned to look back at her.

"Control yourselves, guys. Time to bug her car," Danylo said.

The team broke into Liza Trofimova's Porsche. Hrisha stood guard some distance away from the car in case she decided to come back for some reason. Danylo oversaw the operation from the Skoda, using a radio to communicate with Hrisha and Serhii. Serhii got into the driver's seat of Liza's car and planted a wire just underneath the passenger seat. The whole thing took a couple minutes at most. The wire was sound-activated, and the device would immediately auto-dial a pre-programmed phone number. When someone picked up the phone, they could listen to and record what was happening in the car.

Slava "Bot," a top hacker on the Desperados team, was at their base in Kotsiubynske. Bot had taught the rest of the team how to use the spying hardware and software they'd been given and was in charge of making sure that everything was working in that department.

After Serhii and Bot checked that the wire in Liza's car was working, Bot texted Danylo that everything was set, and Danylo radioed to the rest of the team: "Let's wrap it up." Now all they had to do was wait to hear what Liza had to say.

That same morning, just around corner, another Desperados squad was parked by the main building of the University. Sasha, Vova, and Andrii had a different task. Unlike his sister, Trofimov's son Anton was almost always accompanied by security guards. Sasha, in charge of his group, decided it would be better to watch him for a couple days to identify his friends both in and out of university, where he hangs out, and, if possible, document all this on camera. They would then use this information to decide on their next move.

A Lexus LX470 stopped in front of the university building around 08:05. A heavyset man got out of the front seat, looked around to make sure there were no threats, and carefully opened the back door. Everything about this show seemed arrogant and contemptuous toward other university students and professors. Out of the opened door stepped Anton Trofimov. Dressed in expensive brands like his sister, he had a pretty face and a glamorous haircut.

Sasha told Andrii and Vova to follow Anton. "Right up until he enters his classroom. Take pictures of the people he's talking to, but be careful, you must remain unnoticed. Got it? I'll park the car somewhere nearby and will wait for you there."

"Got it, we'll be in touch," said Andrii. The two set out following Anton Trofimov, pretending to be students.

Sasha parked the VW in the courtyard of a residential building nearby and walked back to the university, hoping to get a closer look at the Lexus Anton arrived in. Meanwhile, Andrii and Vova got into the university without trouble: Bot had forged student ID cards for them as the plan had shaped up, so they could enter and exit the main building of the Taras Shevchenko National University whenever they wanted.

***

Meanwhile, Danylo and his group returned to the base in Kotsiubynske.

"Hey Bot, has Liza gone online yet?" Danylo asked as they arrived.

"All quiet so far, but I heard from Sasha, he said everything was alright on their end, Vova and Andrii were trailing Anton at the university."

"Cool, let's wait. 'He that shall endure unto the end, the same shall be saved.' Ever heard that?"

"Heard it ages ago from an old hag," Bot said, smirking and staring at the screen of his laptop, glad to be able to make Danylo feel like an old fart.

The phone being used to transmit recordings from the wire in Liza's car rang about twenty minutes later.

"Danylo, Liza is online!" Bot yelled.

Over deep house music playing in the background, Liza Trofimova said in her sweet voice, "Hey honey, I just finished at university now, going to get a coffee with Kseniia and then to work out. Want to get dinner together? I have good news, daddy sorted out my internship in Brussels." And after a brief pause, "Okay, great, see you there at nine. I'll have no underwear on. Have a nice day! Don't forget to book a table!" She hung up.

"She's real hot, this Liza," Bot told Danylo. "I feel like we're gonna have a lot of fun with her." Excitement was palpable in his voice.

"Yeah, we definitely won't be bored. Now we need to find out who this guy is, and why her dad was so keen to get her that internship in Brussels. They must be planning something big, or maybe just carrying out someone's orders. I have a hunch about who might be behind this. Gotta call Kostia."

Danylo and Kostia agreed to meet in one of Levchenko's bars. There were hardly any people there when Danylo arrived; the place usually didn't get busy until later in the evening. Kostia's bodyguards took Danylo to the VIP room in the back of the bar.

"Hey Kostia. Got some interesting information about Trofimov's daughter," Danylo said.

"Hello Danylo. Good news. Let's hear it," Kostia replied. The two of them were alone in the room. There was a platter of sushi and a hookah in front of Kostia. He wolfed the sushi down as Danylo spoke.

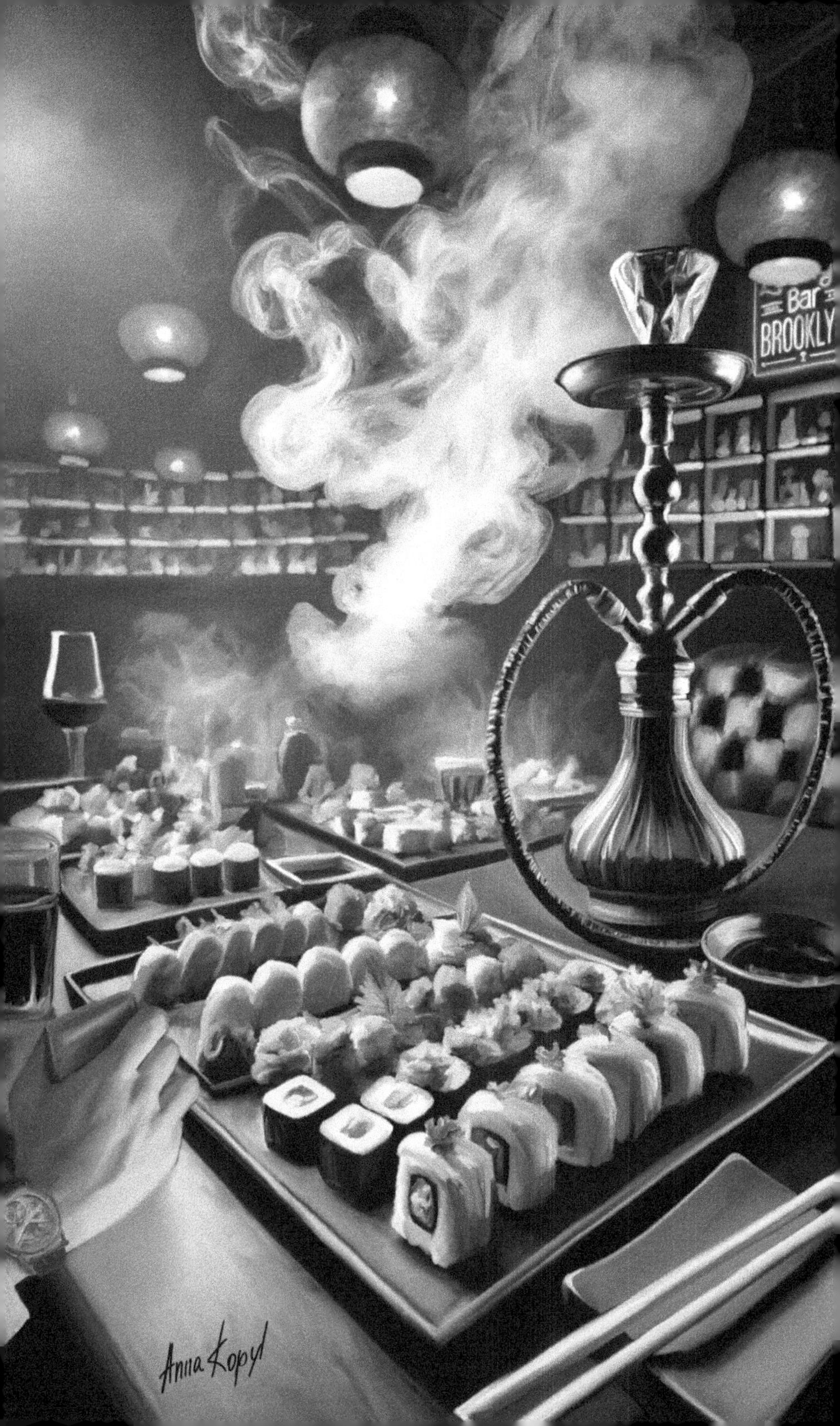
Bar
BROOKLY
Anna Kopyl

"Liza is going to do an internship in Brussels."

"More details, please."

"That's what she said when she was on the phone with her boyfriend – or just someone she's fucking. Or maybe it was a Russian operative."

"By the way man, help yourself to the sushi, or the hookah."

"Thanks. Let me finish first. She's meeting this guy for dinner tonight. He didn't seem to say much, but they must be fucking, because she told him she won't be wearing underwear."

"Woah, an unexpected turn of events!" Kostia gasped. "As far as I knew, she hasn't been seeing anyone for the past couple months."

"That's what I thought! I saw that in the dossier we got from you. That's why I wanted to tell you about this."

When Danylo told Kostia the name of the restaurant where Liza had dinner reservations that evening, Kostia said that a friend of his knew the hostess there, and promised to find out which table Liza and her boyfriend would be sitting at. "You guys can plant a wire at their table or somewhere near," he added.

"No problem, we got it!" Danylo replied.

"Danylo, you guys are doing a great job. Stay in touch. I've got to go, but you can stay, tell the guys to meet you here, have some food, smoke some hookah, and I'll be in touch in the next couple hours with further instructions."

Kostia patted Danylo's shoulder and left. Danylo called Serhii and Hrisha, and after the three had eaten and had a coffee, they left for the restaurant where Liza's date was happening. They parked a block away from the restaurant and waited for a call from Kostia or one of his men. The call came forty minutes later.

"Danylo, it's Paco. I just got here. Are you far? I'll order us something to drink," Paco was one of Kostia's guys. Danylo heard and intuited the plan.

"I'll be there in ten."

"Cool, see you then."

When Danylo came in, he saw Paco at a tucked-away table for two, in the very corner of the restaurant. Paco was beaming with joy, but there was also something cunning about his face. He shook Danylo's hand, "Glad to see you."

"Likewise," replied Danylo.

"I'll tell you what's going to happen. Video- and sound-recording devices has already been installed. It's working. I'll tell you where it is, and when we leave, I'll give you access to the recording. This is the table Liza and her friend will be sitting at. Just listen to me, don't look around or anything. Don't stare, just nod if you understand."

Danylo nodded.

"A minicam that can also record sound is on a shelf just above your head. It's inside the Cuban woman figurine," Paco smiled like a cat that has just gobbled up a delicious fresh fish.

"I've always wanted to go to Cuba," Danylo said.

"Me too man, would love to go there. I think that's it for now, I'll give you the USB drive when we're outside, and then you're in charge. Good luck!"

"As Che Guevara used to say, *hasta la victoria siempre*."

Danylo and Paco left the restaurant, which – not coincidentally – was called Che. Danylo, Serhii, and Hrisha moved the car to a parking lot outside the nearby grocery store. They installed the software from the USB that Paco had given Danylo onto their laptop and sent the files to Bot, back at the base in Kotsiubynske, so that he too could monitor what was happening. It was 8:24pm by the time they were done. All they had to do now was wait for Liza and her boyfriend to arrive.

The couple got to the restaurant around 9:10pm. He was in his early to mid-thirties, tall and well-built. He wore a black leather jacket, jeans, and a pair of Gucci sneakers, and looked wealthy and successful, which made sense given Liza's status. For a while, it seemed that the team wouldn't find anything of interest. Liza and her date smiled at each other and joked around with their server. They ordered a grilled seabream and a crisp Chilean wine and talked about the mutual friends who had introduced them to each other, about holidays in Havana, and about how fitting it was that they were having dinner in a restaurant named after Cuba's famous revolutionary Che Guevara who had helped liberate the sunny island from the ruthless dictator Fulgencio Batista. Anyone with even a superficial knowledge of history could easily grasp the connections here: Cuba, Russia, Russia's Federal Security Service, communism, being recruited by special services. Danylo, for one, thought these connections were meaningful and not accidental. When the couple finished eating, their conversation finally turned to the matters that so interested the Desperados group.

"Liza, tell me about Brussels, will you?" said the man. "You know there's someone eager to hear from you."

"Don't worry Yehor, everything's going according to plan. I'll leave for Belgium in a month. Everything with the internship's been settled. Laurent Mollé is sending the paperwork through today or tomorrow."

"I always knew I could trust you, Liza. Let's toast to your family and your success at the European Parliament!"

"Thank you Yehor, I'll gladly toast to that!"

Danylo felt relieved: finally, his work was starting to pay off. The fog of uncertainty started to lift, and the Desperados group now had a clear sense of direction. After a few minutes talking about other stuff, Liza circled back to her Brussels trip.

"As far as I know, I'll go to France first, where I'll meet Laurent's people and spend a couple of days in the Mollé family's summer house, right?"

"That's right. But just one thing: the 'summer house' is actually a castle. Brittany is stunning, I think you'll love it. You must have oysters while you're there! And make a trip to Rennes."

"Don't you worry about it, honey, I'll make the most of it."

"Liza, darling, I know. I'm not actually worried. And besides, you'll be in the company of real professionals. Anyway, should we continue this conversation in a more private setting? I have a French red from the 2000 vintage at mine that I wanted you to try."

"I'd love to try it. I told my family I'd be meeting my classmates at a club and would stay over at a friend's house," Liza said, holding her wine glass and looking into her lover's eyes.

Yehor asked for the bill and Danylo perked up. He knew that for that evening's operation to be considered a success they had to find out where Yehor lived.

"Serhii, let's go," Danylo said, "we have to follow them! We'll wait for them to leave the restaurant and catch them on the way out."

Their car was parked just a couple minutes away from the restaurant. Danylo called Bot while they drove.

"Bot, did you save the recording? Is the quality good?"

"Hey Danylo, yes, it's perfect. I'm just splicing together the most interesting parts of the conversation."

"Great, we'll be back in an hour or two. Can you make a tape with the most interesting stuff for Kostia while we're gone?" Danylo asked, proud of what he and his team had accomplished that evening.

They pulled up in front of the restaurant and saw Liza and Yehor laughing together outside, waiting for their taxi. When it arrived and the couple got in, Danylo, Hrisha, and Serhii tailed it in their car. They made sure to keep their distance so as not to attract attention. Danylo knew that they were dealing with professionals. The Desperados group was still new to all this and had to learn on the fly. The taxi stopped by a luxury apartment block not far from the Klovska metro station in central Kyiv. Danylo sent Hrisha to follow Liza and Yehor and see which section of the building they entered. Outside, Hrisha waited to see lights turn on in one of the flats above. He couldn't say for sure that it was Liza and Yehor's, but at least the group now knew where to focus their attention.

Danylo called Kostia on the way back to the Kotsiubynske base and agreed to meet him there. The way the day had gone made Danylo think the future would be full of events and surprises. He thought about Liza Trofimova as their car glided through the Kyiv night. Somewhere inside himself, he felt a soft spot growing for her.

***

After circling around the main building of the Taras Shevchenko National University and the nearby Shevchenko Park, Sasha didn't see the Lexus that brought Trofimov's son Anton to the university. He decided to kill some time in the park and bought a newspaper. He had long hours of waiting ahead of him until Anton's classes were over or he'd decide to play truant and leave. Sasha was always restless and hated waiting around. Andrii and Vova were at the university with strict instructions to never let Anton out of sight. Sasha finally settled at the café in the park, looking solemn and nervous. He'd had three coffees and was refreshing his Facebook feed over and over when he got a phone call from Andrii.

"Anton is leaving the university and seems in a rush, we're watching him." Andrii said.

"Great! Follow him! Have you seen the Lexus with his security guards?"

"We haven't, he's on his own and seems to be hurrying to a meeting."

"Right," Sasha said. "I'll go get the car and wait in the parking lot by the university. Let me know if anything happens. Tell Vova to message me on WhatsApp."

"No problem, got you."

After Anton Trofimov left the university, he walked up the Volodymyrska Street to the National Opera Theater and went into a small Japanese restaurant nearby. Andrii and Vova didn't follow him inside but texted Sasha an update on his whereabouts. Anton seemed anxious, even irritated. He smoked a cigarette on his way to the restaurant, though he didn't normally smoke, and kept calling someone on his phone. Sasha, Andrii, and Vova decided that Sasha should be the one to follow Anton inside. After trailing him around the university all morning, the other two might be recognized. The restaurant was called Nagatomo's. It was a small, uncrowded space, with a couple of tourists, seemingly Brits, sitting in one of the booths and Anton and the man he was meeting sitting in another. Sasha slid into the booth next to theirs, with his back to them as they talked animatedly.

"Anton, you have to realize that when Ludwig comes back from Stockholm, we won't be able to see each other as often. I hope you know what I mean."

"Denys, I understand," Anthon responded, "but I'm asking you to think about it again. Don't burn this bridge. Let's at least stay friends! I wouldn't trust this Swedish shmuck if I were you."

"Let's not start throwing insults around. Anton, I get it, you're young and hot-blooded, it's hard for you to control your emotions. But he's not a shmuck. He's a leading IT expert, and these long work trips are part of his job, and I have to be okay with it. We're in a serious relationship and we're going to move to the US soon, where we won't have to hide it and where we'll be able to live a normal, full life. You're so young, and this is just an infatuation, it'll pass soon. And besides, what will your dad think when he finds out about me? And what will happen to me if he does? It's probably better to not think about it…"

"You know," Anton said, pausing to take a breath, "I'm glad I got to know you. And I'm especially glad you're my professor, so you have no choice but to keep seeing me for the rest of the term. But please, at least know that I wish you well." Anton said, then got up and left the restaurant.

The other guy, Denys, kept sat there, staring blankly into the cup of coffee in front of him. A few moments later he seemed to regain his composure, paid for his coffee and anxiously walked back to the university. Sasha, stunned by everything he had just heard, knew he had just struck gold.

***

Both of the Desperado teams met with Kostia and his people at the Kotsiubynske base late that night. The situation was developing rapidly, and they had to agree on their next steps together. Kostia invited Danylo and Sasha to join him in a separate room. After each of them told him about the action that day, Kostia said, "Here's what I'm hearing: Trofimov has a whole bunch of weak points we can use to make the corrupt snake writhe in pain. There's almost too much drama. His daughter is likely involved with the Russian secret service, his son is gay, and Trofimov himself is elbow-deep in corruption. Incredible. I'll meet with Levchenko tomorrow morning and see what he wants us to do next.

Kostia told the guys to get some sleep and meet back at the base at nine in the morning.

∗∗∗

Just after seven the following morning, a brand-new buffed Audi Q7 drove through Koncha-Zaspa, just outside of Kyiv, home to Ukraine's most famous and successful politicians, government officials, and business owners. Kostia was in the passenger seat, his driver at the steering wheel. They stopped in front of one of the chic mansions, and Kostia got out, walked up to the gate, and rang the intercom. The house and grounds behind the gate were enormous. Behind the brick walls was a swimming pool, a shooting range, a gym, and countless other amenities.

All this belonged to Levchenko, or rather his wife – at least on paper. Kostia was invited to come in and was taken to Levchenko's study, where he was asked to wait a few minutes and offered coffee and breakfast. Kostia politely refused the food but said yes to the coffee. He looked at the bookshelves lining the walls of Levchenko's office. He was dressed simply, not too formally: a black leather Hugo Boss jacket, a grey Moncler polo, classic dark blue jeans, and an Hublot watch – a gift from Levchenko. Kostia has been working for him for 15 years. They'd met when Kostia and the guys he'd been running with stole a car belonging to Levchenko's business partner's son, a 2003 Bentley Continental.

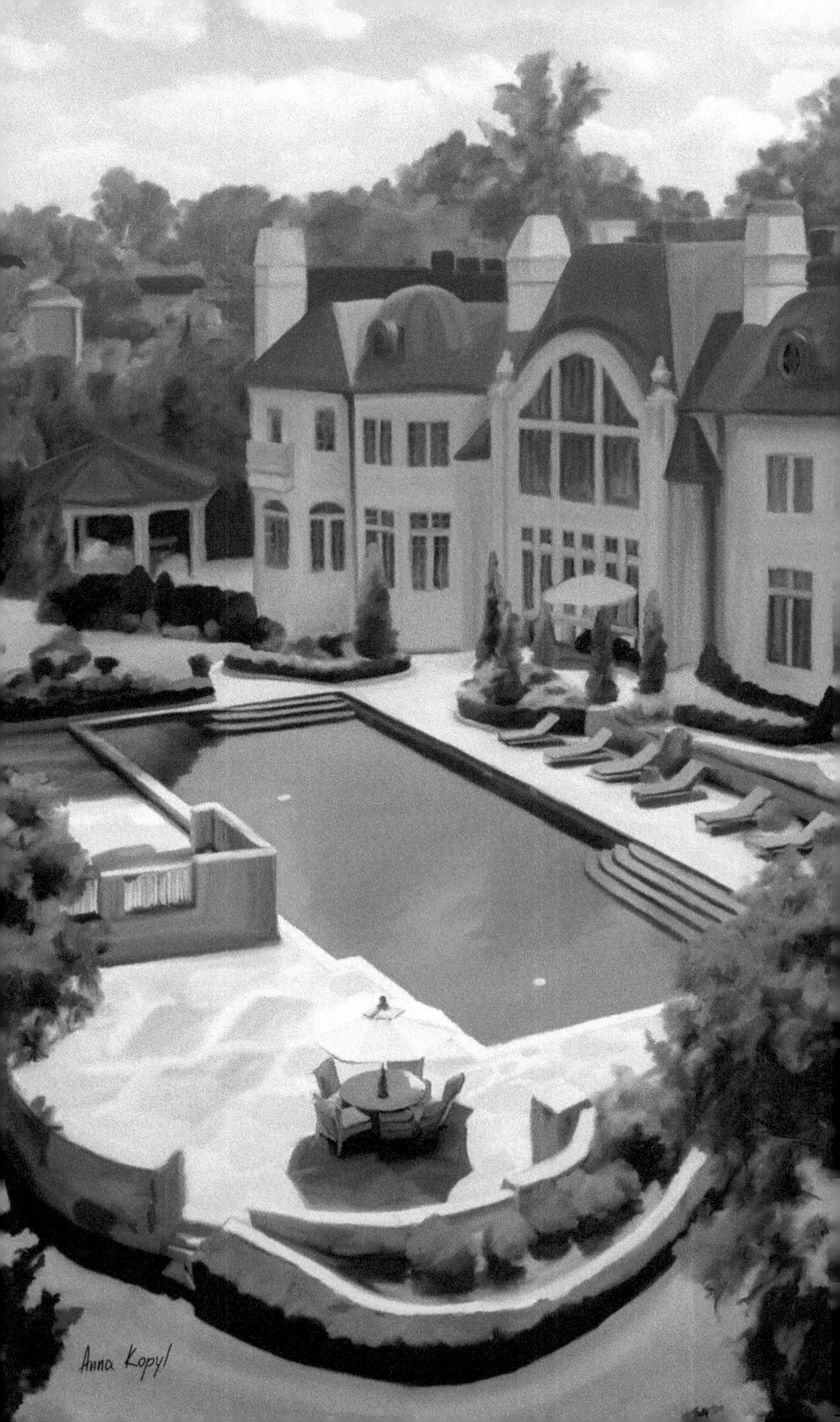
Anna Kopyl

They'd been planning to take the car to Russia, where they already had a buyer lined up. But when Kostia found out that Levchenko was personally involved in trying to locate the car, he had made a wise decision – after all, Levchenko was even then already one of the most influential people in all of Kyiv. Kostia personally took the car to Levchenko's office and apologized to Levchenko, who thought it was a courageous thing to do. When Levchenko's left hand, Zurab Kvirkveliia, was shot and killed several months later, Levchenko got in touch with Kostia and offered him the job. Kostia immediately agreed. Eventually he established a network of people to work for him under Levchenko that he could rely on and trust. The workforce had only grown over the years, aided by the growth of Levchenko's business ventures.

Over the fifteen years that Kostia worked for him, Levchenko transformed from a criminal authority and a promising businessman into someone welcomed into and respected by the Ukrainian elite: a millionaire, politician, and philanthropist. Of course, he was not without sin. You could probably write an entire book about his vices and sins, but these were outweighed by the fact that he always kept his word and was fair and just in demanding situations and conflicts. This earned him the respect not only of his staff, but everyone around him. His Achilles' heel had always been his insatiable attraction to women. He had three kids with his first wife and a young son with his second and current wife Marharyta. An unknown number of lovers had also borne an unknown number of kids. To put it diplomatically, he was big-hearted man.

The doors of the study opened just as Kostia was finishing his coffee.

Levchenko was glowing with joy, checking his Patek Philippe watch as he came. "Good morning Kostia! I was told yesterday that we're seeing some success. I'm happy with what we have so far; tell the guys to keep doing what they're doing, they're doing a great job. Are you hungry? Our cook makes these amazing pancakes, you should try them." Wearing a black Brioni suit, he looked like he had important meetings ahead of him that day.

"Good morning. Thanks for the offer, but I'll have to pass on the pancakes," Kostia said. "I had breakfast before I came, but I'd love another coffee. The Desperados group really did a great job. You were right about them. I don't want to jinx it, but I believe in them. I wanted to ask you what we should do next."

"I'll have a coffee with you. Just a second, let me just call a maid. Let's leave Liza alone for now. Don't touch her. Not a good time to get mixed up with the Russian secret service. Look into this professor who's fucking Anton. Find out who he is and what he's up to," Levchenko ordered. "We'll then have to blackmail him, so he cooperates with us. We need a video of him and Anton, and we'll need to send it to Anton's dad. That will put an end to his political ambitions. It would also be good to figure out what Panchyshyn's deal is. There are rumors that he's involved in drug trafficking in the

ATO zone[1], amphetamine. Is that clear enough for a direction?" he asked. "Let's wrap up for now, I don't have a lot of time."

"Understood. I'll keep you posted," Kostia replied. He shook Levchenko's hand and left.

Kostia thought about his next moves as he drove from Koncha-Zaspa to Kotsiubynske. When he arrived, he briefed the members of the Desperados group on what each of them was to do next. He split the group into two teams. The first included Sasha, Andrii and Bot, who would stay in Kyiv and try to catch Anton Trofimov and his professor red-handed. The second team – Danylo, Serhii, Hrisha and Vova – were to travel around the Kyiv and Zhytomyr regions and the ATO zone in the east of Ukraine to dig deeper into Panchyshyn's dealings. Their first destination was Irpin, just outside of Kyiv. Panchyshyn's NGO worked closely with the Irpin City Council, and the city council had helped it with funding on more than one occasion. The NGO also appeared to be closely tied with the Korosten City Council, so Korosten would be the second stop for Danylo's team. After Korosten, the team would take a trip to the city of Yasynuvata in the ATO zone. Yasynuvata, controlled by Donetsk People's Republic terrorists, was at the epicenter of fighting between Ukrainian forces and their Russian occupiers.

---

[1] The Anti-Terrorist Operation, or ATO, is a term used from 2014 to 2018 by the media, the government of Ukraine and the Organization for Security and Co-operation in Europe (OSCE) to identify combat actions in parts of Donetsk and Luhansk oblasts against Russian military forces and pro-Russian separatists.

There was no time to waste. The teams started working on their assignments as soon as Kostia's talk finished. Bot scoured the internet to find everything he could about Anton Trofimov's professor, Denys Doronin. Doronin worked in the Department of Theory of State and Law at the Taras Shevchenko National University in Kyiv. He was active on social media, meaning that Bot could easily access all sorts of information about him: what car he drove (a dark red Mazda 6), who his parents and friends were, where he liked hanging out. Doronin enjoyed showing his private life off online, and the habit was now backfiring on him. It must have never crossed his mind that his social media would be a golden vein to secret services, criminal gangs, and all sorts of scammers. There he was, doubly unlucky that the Desperados group was something of a hybrid between a special service and a gang.

Doronin often worked out at a gym in central Kyiv. Bot came up with a plan: he would go to the gym while Doronin was working out and ask for his phone under the pretext that he needed to make an urgent call, and his phone was dead. He would then install the Spy's Eye spying software on Doronin's phone, which would allow the Desperados team to see everything Doronin did on his phone remotely, on their devices. Sasha quickly agreed to Bot's plan.

The team's first task was to find out when Doronin usually went to the gym. The day after the meeting, Sasha and Andrii waited in front of the university building where Doronin worked. When he was done teaching around two in the afternoon, he left for home with Sasha and Andrii in tow. At 5:30pm, he left home and headed straight to the gym. Bingo. Doronin seemed to aim to be at the gym for six. It was a Monday, so Sasha and Andrii figured that they would find him there again on Wednesday and Friday.

The team moved on to the next stage of their operation. On Wednesday, Bot waited in the parking lot for Doronin to arrive at the gym. Bot wore a brand-new tracksuit, Nike sneakers, a pair of Calvin Klein glasses, and had a trendy haircut to match. The goal was to make him look smart. He was to pretend to be an IT professional who had just moved to Kyiv from Lviv and was looking to make friends.

Sasha and Andrii called Bot as Doronin left his apartment. Everything went exactly to plan. Bot had no trouble getting Doronin to believe the story he fabricated. Doronin took the bait and said that he also had friends in IT and could introduce Bot if he was interested. Everything went down like clockwork.

After consulting with Kostia, Sasha and his team decided that it was too risky to try and install Spy's Eye on Doronin's phone at the gym; the work would be easier in a more casual and relaxed environment, at a party or in a club maybe, when the unsuspecting Doronin let his guard down after a few cocktails. That would be the time for Bot to act.

Bot was at the gym by 5:40pm on Friday, waiting for the target. Doronin came in a bit later than usual, around

6:15pm. Nervous of squandering the opportunity, Bot approached him almost immediately.

"Hey Denys! How's it going man?" Bot asked. "Can you spot me while I bench-press?"

"Oh hey! Yeah sure, no sweat. Thank God it's Friday, couldn't wait for the weekend," Doronin said. "Honestly, this has been a horrible week. But what about you? Getting used to your new life in the capital?"

"It's tough, I'm not used to the pace – takes ages to get places, traffic's killing me. But yeah, getting used to it, think I'll be alright in a month or two."

The two stood over the bench. "How are things going with your personal life?" Doronin asked. "Aren't you going to bring your girlfriend over from Lviv?"

"I don't have a girlfriend. To be honest, I never had a long-term relationship," Bot said, improvising. "Never even felt in love. Us IT guys are a particular type of people. I must've not met the girl I'm meant for yet…"

Doronin seemed satisfied with Bot's reply. A thought crossed his mind of the possibility of having an affair with the lonely guy from Lviv. After four sets of bench presses each, Bot asked Doronin what he was doing that night, and if he wanted to go clubbing. Bot had read the moment right, suggesting what was already on Doronin's mind. Surprised by the coincidence, Doronin cheerfully replied, "Why not?"

"A DJ I know is playing at Drunken Monkey tonight, some friends of mine were asking if I wanted to join them there," he went on. "And by the way, a few owners of big IT firms will be there, I'll introduce you. If you want me too, of course."

"So, what time should we meet?"

"Let's say 11pm outside of the club. Come well-rested and in good mood – we'll party until dawn! I need to relax," Doronin said, "I've been so tense lately."

"Great, I'll be there! Don't be late," Bot managed a fake smile and pretended to be pleased with the plan.

Bot felt anxious and disgusted with himself as he left the gym. He didn't have anything against gay people, but he wasn't particularly thrilled to be acting like he was into anyone, either. Besides, the rest of the Desperados group were already making fun of him behind his back. He couldn't wait for the operation to be over.

Doronin arrived at Drunken Monkey ahead of time, soon after 10pm, to meet his old friend Fedia Berlin. Fedia was a dealer of everything from heroin to cocaine. He'd been selling drugs in Kyiv for the past five years, paying his dues to law enforcement regularly and always on time. In turn, they left him alone to pursue his business. In fact, his business improved after he began cooperating with cops three years ago, when they first found out about his dealings. In Ukraine, as in other post-Soviet countries, the drug business was intertwined with law enforcement even more so than with criminal gangs, so if you wanted to deal large volumes, you had to cooperate with law enforcement officials. Fedia, for instance, had to dole out the lion's share of his profits to the cops. He modelled his business after any other organization: he had sales agents and supervisors, operators and stock managers. Meanwhile, the drug business boomed in Kyiv and other major Ukrainian cities, thanks to the Telegram messenger and a network of hideouts. All you had to do was join a Telegram group and send a message listing the drugs you wanted to the group's admins. They would tell you the price and payment details, and after you paid, you were sent an address where you could pick up the goods. For example, 72 Patrice Lumumba Street, fourth floor, under the ashtray. And along those lines, Fedia managed to make a decent living, investing his profits into real estate.

"It's been too long, Denys!" Fedia called, as Doronin walked in. "How's work going?"

Doronin hugged his friend, "Guten Abend, Fedia! So happy to see you. I've not been doing that great but, you know, everything that happens is for the best. I've been a bit depressed lately, so that's why I called you. Don't know anyone better than you to cheer me up."

"I got the goods. Top quality, just for you. A bump before we head in?"

"Let's do it, get ready to party!"

By the time Bot got to the club, Doronin and Fedia had sampled the cocaine twice. Doronin had convinced Fedia to stay out, and the night was off to a promising start. Bot joined the two of them, and they met up with a group of Doronin's friends who were already there. There was a dozen or more people at their table –

everyone drank and chatted and waited for midnight to strike, when the club's headlining act, a DJ from London, would start his set. Bot waited for Doronin to get drunk so he could ask to borrow his phone and install the spying software on it. Andrii, another member of the Desperados group, was also in the club if Bot needed help. Sasha waited in a car nearby, overseeing the entire operation. Doronin and Fedia were high and were drinking whisky. Bot also drank but refused the offers of cocaine. Feeling out of his depth, he stepped outside and called Sasha, panicked.

"Sasha, it's not going great, I don't think our plan's going to work. Maybe we should try another time, or come up with another plan?"

"Are you out of your goddamn mind?" Sasha yelled into the phone, "No! We have to do this tonight. Do what you want, but the software has to be installed on Denys's phone tonight. Go back to the club, take a hit of cocaine with them, or whatever they're getting high on, act like you're part of their group, but don't lose your composure. Remember: first and foremost, you've got a mission, and our reputation – and the fate of the whole enterprise – is in your hands. Don't let us down. I believe in you."

"Fuck, Sasha, this is a total nightmare..." Bot said, desperately. He took a breath. "But alright, alright, I'll do what I can."

"Go take a bump and you'll feel more confident. Okay, get back there. Stop calling attention to yourself," Sasha said and hung up.

Bot regained his composure, returned to the club, and headed straight for the table where Doronin sat with his friends. Neither Doronin nor Fedia were there, so Bot circled the dance floor. He found Fedia with two women clinging to him. He'd got them high on cocaine in the club's bathroom. Doronin danced next to them like no one was watching. Bot thought that he must have also taken extasy.

Bot walked toward Doronin and yelled over the music, "Denys, do you have any coke left? I want to take a bump, I'm bored of just drinking whisky!"

"Of course! Let's go to the bathroom. Took you ages to get there – *I don't want it, I don't need it*," Doronin mocked Bot.

After the two had their fix of cocaine in the bathroom, they returned to the table and drank more whisky. Forty minutes later, they did it all again. At almost 3am, Fedia suggested leaving in an hour or so to go to an afterparty at an acquaintance's house. Doronin said he'd go after his friend's set. He pulled one of the guys at their table away to join him on the dance floor. Bot was anxious. He knew it was time for him to act. Andrii would occasionally appear in his periphery, signaling that the time was ripe and that he had a job to get done. Bot resolved to ask Doronin for his phone the next time that he saw him. When Denys returned to the table with his friend, Bot sprang into action.

"Hey Denys, can I have your phone, mine just died and I have to make an urgent call!"

"No phone calls tonight! We're partying hard! We still have the afterparty ahead of us, remember? No way I'm giving you my phone! You'll make your call and abandon us! Good thing yours is out of charge."

Though Bot hadn't expected the response, the cocaine had somehow dialed him in, and he understood instinctively that he shouldn't draw attention to the hiccup. He had to be patient and finish what he started.

"Ah the afterparty, of course! Let's call a taxi maybe?"

Zhenia Karavaiiev threw famous parties at his high-tech penthouse on the Obolonska Embankment. These parties were attended by the crème de la crème of Kyiv and the elite of other post-Soviet and Eastern European countries. Zhenia was a famous fashion designer and a sponsor and patron of several major events on Ukraine's fashion calendar. He never had to think about money: his grandfather was a high-ranking official in the Communist Party and had embezzled enough money to sustain at least three generations of progeny.

Doronin and the friend he was dancing with, Fedia and his two ladies, and Bot headed to Zhenia's after they left the club. There weren't many people at Zhenia's, maybe a dozen or so. Zhenia was looking at clothes on the screen of a large projector with about half of the guests, and the rest were couples, making out in various corners of the apartment. Zhenia was bisexual and frequently hosted orgies in his apartment. He jokingly referred to them as Roman Games. Zhenia followed Fedia and Doronin into one of the rooms in his flat, where Fedia sold him a couple grams of cocaine and a dozen MDMA pills. Then Fedia opened a bottle of champagne, took the two women he came with by the arms, and led them to an upstairs bedroom. Meanwhile, Bot joined Doronin and his friend from the club at a granite counter in the kitchen, where they drank whisky. Bot made his second attempt to get Doronin's phone; this time, he agreed. Bot left the kitchen, shut himself in the bathroom, and installed Spy's Eye on the phone. By the time he was done fifteen minutes later, the kitchen was empty. Bot went up the stairs in search of Doronin and peered into one of the bedrooms, whose doors were open. Inside, Denys was making out with his friend from the club. Bot knew what he had to do: he pulled out his phone out and took pictures. Doronin and his friend didn't see or hear Bot – loud music boomed through the apartment – and he went back downstairs. He gave Doronin's phone to Zhenia and quietly left the apartment. He walked for a while, still shaky, and called Sasha. The operation was finally over, and Bot couldn't have been more pleased with the outcome.

Sasha picked Bot up. They got coffees at a gas station and went over everything that had happened during the night. Bot was exhausted and fell asleep as soon as they got back in the car. He got another few hours of sleep once they arrived back to the base in Kotsiubynske, but soon it was time to start on the next phase of the operation. Bot checked whether Spy's Eye was working on Doronin's phone and found that the software was working perfectly. Anton Trofimov had called Doronin a dozen times over the course of the night and sent him two texts and three Instagram messages. By the time Kostia arrived at the base, the team had decided that it was time to put the photos Bot had taken at Zhenia's apartment to use. They wanted to send the photos to Anton Trofimov, hopefully encouraging him to avenge his broken heart and unrequited love by blackmailing Doronin using the photos Bot took. The goal was then to get Anton to tell Doronin that he would share the photos with his Swedish boyfriend, which would threaten Doronin's American dream. In order to avoid this, Doronin would have to agree to a romantic rendezvous with Anton. All the Desperados had to do was figure out how to make it all happen – in short, how to make Anton do what they wanted him to do. Their ultimate goal was to record Anton and Doronin at the site of their meeting, and send the video to Anton's father, Hennadii Trofimov. Such compromising material involving Trofimov's son and his university professor would inevitably lead Trofimov to agree to Levchenko's demands.

***

Meanwhile, Danylo and three other members of the Desperados group roved the city of Irpin, not far from the Desperados' base in Kotsiubynske. Quiet and comfortable Irpin, home to some 50,000 residents, famous for its parks and clean air. On the morning in question, the Desperados' Land Cruiser Prado was parked on one of the city's central streets, with Serhii, Hrisha, and Vova inside. Danylo stood outside, away from the cruiser, waiting for Stepan Pysarenko, a developer and member of the Irpin City Council,

Levchenko's old friend and business partner. Pysarenko was twenty or so years older than Levchenko, but he kept up with the times and knew all the latest trends no worse – and at times better – than younger generations. He was cunning and had a sixth sense when it came to money-making opportunities. As with many people around him, it was that quality that Levchenko particularly valued in Pysarenko.

Danylo waited for ten minutes or so before a slate grey Toyota Camry stopped in front of him.

A big man in the driver's seat said, "Good afternoon! Are you Danylo?"

"That's me."

"I'm here on Stepan Pysarenko's behalf. Get in, I'll take you to his office."

Without a second thought, Danylo got into the back of the car, which took him to Pysarenko's office. Pysarenko was a very careful man. Irpin being a small city where everyone knows everything about everyone else, Pysarenko didn't want Levchenko's people to be seen. It could turn out to damage both of them, so better to be safe than sorry. Pysarenko's enemies closely followed his every movement and kept track of who he was meeting and doing business with.

Pysarenko's driver took Danylo to a small, modern business center. Danylo took the elevator to the third floor, where he was greeted by Pysarenko's secretary Olia. Olia wore heels and a short skirt. Her white shirt had a deep neckline and showed off what Danylo thought must be silicone breasts. The silicone injections would have been paid for by Pysarenko, who was – not coincidentally – her lover. Pysarenko's wife knew and didn't mind. Olia took Danylo to Pysarenko's office, a spacious room with a large oak meeting table in the middle of the room, a crystal chandelier, and an enormous leather sofa, where Olia put in her second shift. On the other side of the room, a wall of shelves was full of folders and books. Pysarenko's desk stood in the back. On it sat a large globe made of rare woods and precious metals, and an office chair with a whole range of bells and whistles, like a built-in massage function, was pulled up behind it. There was a bar within easy reach of the chair. It was a classic example of a post-Soviet official's office – the office of someone who knew how to curry favors with their superiors. Pysarenko greeted Danylo at the door to his office with wide-open arms and a huge smile on his old face.

"Good afternoon, Danylo, I've been waiting for you! Would you like a tea or a coffee? Or maybe something stronger?"

"Good afternoon, Mr. Pysarenko. I'll have a coffee if that's alright."

"What would you like, an americano, an espresso? With milk or without?" Olia asked flirtingly. She liked Danylo's perfume.

"An americano with milk, please."

"Got it. Would you like your usual espresso, Mr. Pysarenko?"

"Yes, of course. And pour us two glasses of that Armenian brandy I got from my friend Ashot."

"Mr. Pysarenko, thank you for your kind offer, but I'll say no to the brandy," Danylo said.

"Well, I had to offer… Olia, I'll still take a glass."

Olia smiled, poured Pysarenko his brandy, and left the room to make their coffees.

"Levchenko asked me to check what Common Future, Panchyshyn's NGO, was up to," Pysarenko led in. "There are no leads. Two members of the Irpin City Council from the People's Conscience party are lobbying for Panchyshyn's interests. They've embezzled money from the local budget a couple of times, but not a lot. I would say they're mostly trying to make the NGO more widely known and popular. It's all for show. The real crux of what's happening, though, isn't what they're doing politically or with regards to the NGO…"

"Right, that's what we need. What is it?" Danylo asked, looking Pysarenko in the eye.

"There are rumors that these two members of the city council, Selezniov and Kosinchuk, are dealing – what's it called – amphetamine, a difficult word. Selezniov is the son of the leader of a local gang, who protects their business affairs around here."

"Do you know where they buy the amphetamine? Or do they make it themselves?"

"There are rumors that Panchyshyn and Kosinchuk often travel to somewhere near Yasynuvata, maybe that's where they get it. But I'm not sure."

Danylo spent another twenty minutes talking to Pysarenko and found out more details he wanted to know. A rough plan started to emerge in his mind. His first step would be to get to know Pysarenko's secretary, Olia, better, because she seemed like someone who knew all the town gossip. He would then try to place a tracking device on Kosinchuk's car and to follow his movements.

Danylo said goodbye to Pysarenko and left his office. In the reception area, he asked Olia for her phone number. "Mr. Pysarenko is a busy man," he said, "I don't want to distract him from his work. It would be easier to communicate through you."

"Of course," Olia replied. "Here's my business card, call if you need anything, I'd be glad to help."

"Actually, it's my first time in Irpin. Would you mind if I called you out of hours? Maybe you can recommend somewhere nice for dinner?"

Olia's eyes shone. Danylo knew she'd taken his bait.

"Yes, but don't call too late."

"Deal! Have a nice day. See you soon!"

"Good luck, Danylo!" Olia said as he left the reception.

Danylo met up with the rest of his Irpin crew, and they headed back to Kotsiubynske. They needed Bot to set up a tracking device for Kosinchuk's car and to figure out what to do about Pysarenko's secretary. Kostia would know what to do. Two hours later, Kostia came to meet Danylo at the Kotsiubynske base, and they headed for a walk through the nearby woods, towards a lake. The two exchanged pleasantries and laughed about Bot's anxiety around his mission with Doronin. Danylo began to lay out his plan for the operation in Irpin.

"We'll plant a tracking device on Kosinchuk's car and figure out where their lab is," he explained. "But I have another idea. Pysarenko's secretary might be moving in the same circles as Panchyshyn's cronies, so I think it would be good to take her out for a glass of wine and find out what she knows. I have a feeling she might be useful for us. What do you think?"

"Danylo, admit it, you just want to fuck her!"

"To be honest, I wouldn't say no, but mostly I think she could be an asset to the operation."

"Right, jokes aside. I agree that we should get her on our side, at least for the time being. You shouldn't meet any resistance from Pysarenko, but if you do, I have powerful leverage over him. I'll tell you something if you swear not to spread it round."

"My lips are sealed."

"About two years ago, Levchenko met with Pysarenko at his Irpin office, they had some work matters they needed to figure out together. Afterwards, they drank brandy, and Levchenko offered Pysarenko some cocaine. Anyhow, eventually they both ended up fucking the poor secretary right then and there, while her boyfriend waited in a car outside. She called him and told him she'd be half an hour late because she wanted to catch up with work. Afterwards I think Levchenko and Pysarenko paid for her to go on a holiday in the Dominican Republic."

"Jesus. Didn't expect that."

"Yes, and I forgot to mention: she went to the Dominican Republic with that guy who was waiting for her outside while Levchenko and Pysarenko were fucking her. Danylo, do whatever you want, but get a good scoop for us. I'll give you as much money as you need."

"Deal. I'll call her today and arrange a meeting."

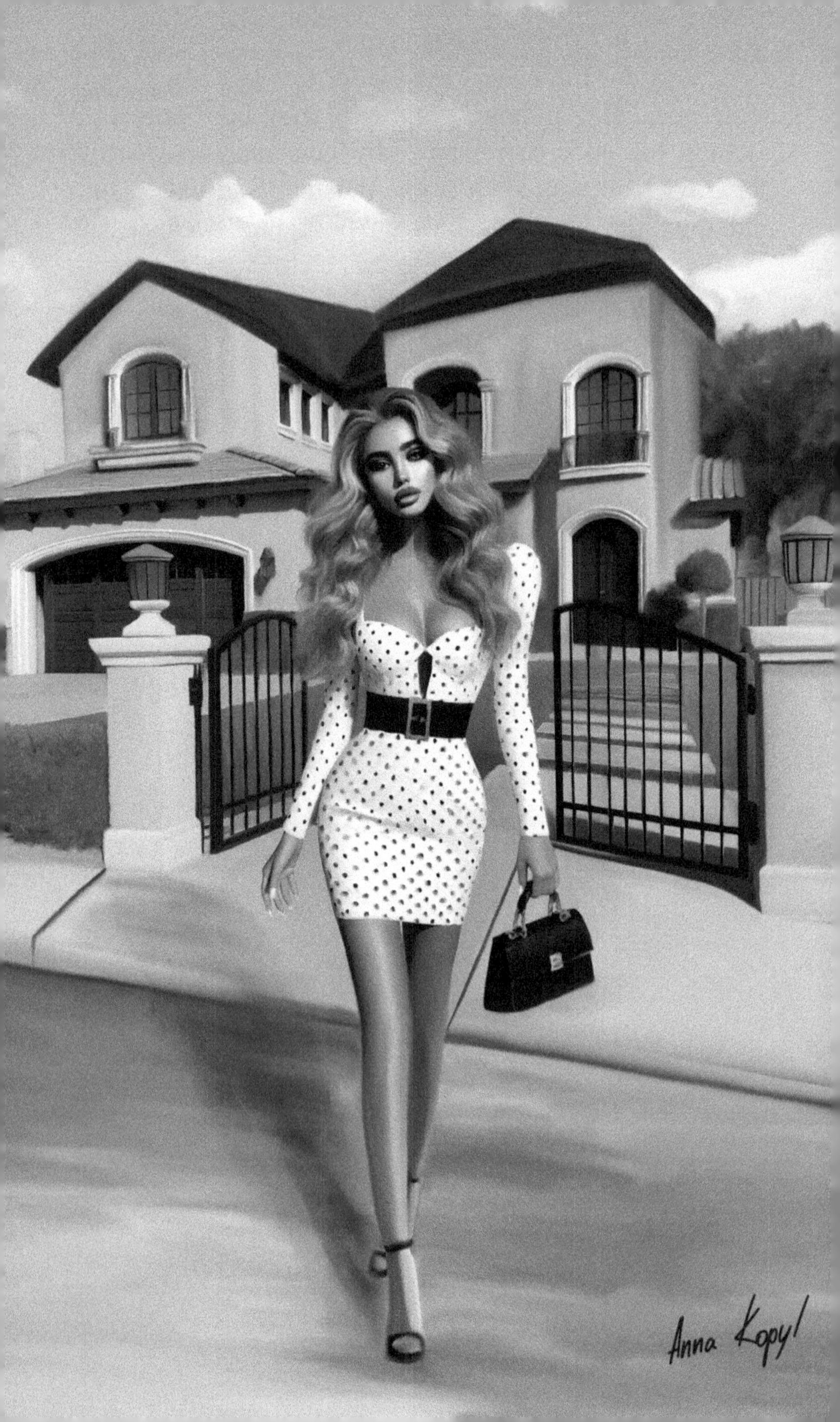
Anna Kopyl

Danylo called Olia around six and asked her out on a date later that night at Grandpa's Garden Resort in the village of Bilohorodka, twenty kilometers outside of Kyiv. Danylo told Olia he'd pick her up at 8:30pm outside her house. Vova was to act as Danylo's driver: they wanted Olia to think Danylo was a big deal and had tons of money to throw around. Meanwhile, Serhii and Hrisha were tasked with planting a tracking device in Kosinchuk's car that same night.

Danylo's Toyota was waiting outside Olia's by 8:25pm. She lived with her parents in a neat two-story house with a pretty garden in Irpin's private residential neighborhood. Olia was twenty minutes late when she stepped out of the gates. She looked gorgeous. Danylo was stunned speechless for a few moments. He hasn't been in a relationship for a while, and suddenly he was faced with someone so beautiful and sexy. Vova was also struck by Olia's looks, but quickly regained composure and got out to open the back door for Olia so she could sit next to Danylo. Olia wore a flattering, closely fitting white and black polka-dot cocktail dress with another deep cut neckline. Her light-brown hair seemed to have a golden tinge to it. She wore black Valentino heels she'd got in Italy and a small, black Michael Kors bag. Her make-up made her look like a movie star, and her intoxicating perfume suited her tan, lithe body. She knew exactly what impression she was making and wanted to say something to alleviate the tension and distract Danylo from ogling her.

"Where are we going, Danylo?" Olia asked.

"Grandpa's Garden. The food there is great, and it's a quiet place, set in a beautiful landscape. I need a break from the noise and the bustle of the big city."

It didn't take them long to get there. Vova stayed in the car, awaiting further instructions. By the time Danylo and Olia were looking at the menu at their table, they were openly flirting with one another.

"Olia, would you prefer meat or fish – and so, red or white wine?" Danylo asked her.

"You're such a know it all! I like that. I think I want to try the grilled salmon, so it'll have to be white for me…"

"Excellent choice! I'll get the lamb chops and some red Georgian wine to go with them."

"You're a real beast," Olia said, looking him in the eye.

"Careful, joking around like that, or my hunting instinct will make me want to eat you."

"Don't scare me like that!" she blushed. "And here's a little secret about me: I love being high on adrenaline."

Both sensed the promise of the night ahead of them. After telling each other about themselves and swapping stories about their lives for a while, Danylo turned the conversation to Irpin and its residents; his main goal that evening, after all, was to see if he could find anything out about Selezniov and Kosinchuk. After they'd each had at least a couple glasses of wine, Danylo started making headway.

"Olia, you seem like someone who knows lots of people. I've heard some talk about Arsen Selezniov, the young and promising business owner, do you by any chance know him?"

"Yes, of course. We went to the same school, he was in the year above me, a real dickhead. But I'm really good friends with his best friend's wife, Svieta Kosinchuk. I've known her for at least ten years."

"Ten years is a long time! How's the Kosinchuk family doing?"

"To be honest, not great. Arsen Selezniov is always egging Dima Kosinchuk on to mess around with girls. They've both had too many affairs. Rumors inevitably reach Svieta Kosinchuk – of course she doesn't like it, they argue and bicker all the time. A few times I thought they'd get divorced. Why are you asking, Danylo? Thinking of looking for a bride and starting a family? Or maybe you've already found one?"

Realizing that Olia couldn't wait to get married, Danylo decided to play along.

"Of course I'm thinking about it… But I'm still looking for the one. Though you never know when you'll meet her, it could happen at any moment. Life is so unpredictable, you know?"

"I one hundred percent agree. The most important thing is not to let that moment go by, or you'll regret it forever. Although you men probably see these things differently. You're not too bothered, this one or that. Or am I wrong?"

"I guess there's some truth in that, but judging everyone by the same yardstick isn't fair either. What about you, Olia? Are you ready to be someone's wife?"

"Depends! It's a big question," Olia became evasive, worried that Danylo would start probing her about her past. Danylo took advantage of her silence and ordered more wine.

"Olia," he started, "I think that anyone who wants to start a family has to first and foremost be mentally – and, ideally, financially – prepared for it. Marriage is first and foremost about responsibility, and willingness to find a compromise. Your husband or wife has to be your friend, your ally who helps you achieve certain goals, rather than stands in your way. We have to be prepared to face both good and bad together. Of course, that's my personal opinion. You might not agree. But look, I'm just being honest with you. I think most people today are obsessed with material wealth and that's the basis of their relationships. I don't think that's quite right."

"Wow, Danylo, you must be a philosopher or something," Olia joked. "You're a pleasant surprise – I didn't expect something like that from you."

"So, you underestimated me?"

"Maybe... Can't quite tell yet."

"I mean, your friend Svieta was after some mythical wealth and now look at her," Danylo went on. "She doesn't know what to do about the pickle she's in. She doesn't want to lose her husband, but she's also not loving all this betrayal. It's a vicious cycle."

"Well, yes. He's constantly lying to her, saying that he's traveling to the frontline and helping our soldiers in the war against the Russians and the separatists. He says it's his civil duty. Meanwhile, he's God knows where and with God knows who. Svieta gets calls from her friends telling her they've seen her husband in this or that restaurant in Kyiv, always with different women."

"How often does he say he go to the ATO zone?" Danylo asked.

"At least twice a month. He and a few other guys from his party work with the Common Future NGO to help the army. I was talking to Svieta just yesterday and she said Dima was about to travel east again in a couple of days."

Bingo! Danylo figured he'd received his share of information for the day, sent a message to Serhii telling him that they had to start tracking Dima Kosinchuk's car immediately, and relaxed into the rest of the evening.

"Olia, it's already late. I've got a suite in this hotel, why don't you stay with me? My driver can take you home tomorrow morning, you'll be able to get to work for ten."

"Sure, but promise me you'll be on your worst behavior. And get us a bottle of wine to take to the room. I promise you'll remember the night for a long time."

"Deal. I'll do everything you want me to. Now why don't you go to the room, and I'll get the wine and join you there in a few minutes? Don't miss me too much."

"Don't take too long or I might change my mind. Us women can be so unpredictable…"

When Olia left, Danylo walked to the car to tell Vova that he'd be staying at the hotel and ask him to come back at 7am sharp. He rushed to the room. The light was on in the bathroom and the rest of the room was shrouded in darkness. Olia was sitting on the enormous bed in the middle of the room, her dress and underwear were lying on the floor. Danylo put the bottle of wine he brought from the restaurant on the table, took off his shirt and walked up to Olia. She undid his belt, then the button and zipper of his jeans. The night was still young.

The two hardly slept all night but woke up to the alarm at 6:30am. Danylo was in a good mood even though he felt exhausted – Olia turned out to be a real expert. He was a bit stunned by how good she was, in fact. He hadn't experienced anything like that in his life.

Vova was waiting for them outside, as agreed. They took Olia home. As soon as she stepped out of the car, Vova turned to Danylo, "Well, how was it?"

"Man, you can't even imagine. She's a real sex machine!"

"Lucky you," Vova said with a hint of bitterness in his voice.

"Yeah, lucky indeed. Don't be a jerk – shouldn't you be glad for your friend? Anyway, drop me off at the Kyiv apartment, then we'll go see Kostia, he should be somewhere in central Kyiv today. I'll call him and arrange a meeting."

While Danylo was with Olia that night, Serhii and Hrisha had planted a tracking device on Dima Kosinchuk's car. Once at the flat, Danylo took a shower, got changed, and hopped back into the car to go straight to the Brooklyn lounge bar (owned by Levchenko) where he was meeting Kostia. The bar was officially closed to customers at that early hour and the staff were still setting up for the day ahead, but Kostia was already there, having a coffee and looking at something on his phone. He smiled his cunning smile when he saw Danylo.

"How was it, James Bond? Did you enjoy it? You're looking kind of shit, Olia must've worn you out. Perk up, Danylo, perk up! The party will repay you for your efforts."

"Hey," Danylo greeted Kostia, "what can I say, she's a real expert. I felt like I was in a porno."

"Good work, good work. Well, I hope you were also at the top of your game."

"Oh, don't you worry about that, man."

"Any useful information?"

"Oh yes. Olia is friends with Dima Kosinchuk's wife, seems like Kosinchuk and co. travel to the ATO zone at least twice a month. Olia said she heard that their next trip is imminent."

"That's great! You killed two birds with one stone: got useful info for the team and had fun yourself. Now stay in touch with her and don't ghost her, but don't get too close with her either. She's a snake if ever I've known one. We can't afford to lose you to her."

"No, no, I get it. Don't worry about it."

"Anyway, focus on Kosinchuk for now and make sure he doesn't leave Irpin unnoticed. I got paperwork sorted so you can enter the ATO zone. As far as I know, Panchyshyn always travels to Donbas with Kosinchuk. Also, to maximize our reach, why don't you and Vova go to Korosten and see what's happening there while Serhii and Hrisha stay in Irpin and monitor the situation there? My people will meet you in Korosten, and you can head east from there. Do you have any questions, concerns, ideas?"

"All good I think, I'll call you if anything comes up!"

Danylo and Vova left for Korosten, some 150 kilometers away from Kyiv, and got there two hours later. They were meeting Ilona Zhdanova and her son Valerii. Ilona was Levchenko's head accountant in the 90s; at the time, she was the cornerstone of his business empire, and one of the most useful people for Levchenko. She was also his lover. There were rumors that her son Valerii was Levchenko's son, and indeed they looked quite alike. Now, Ilona was the deputy director of the state-owned Koros Quarry, a granite-mining firm. Her son owned the largest and most popular club in the area, Planet. Ilona and Valerii met Danylo and Vova in the Ostrovskyi Park in Korosten. Danylo got there a bit before them and was waiting by the Queen Olha monument. Ilona and Valerii arrived fifteen minutes later.

"Good afternoon Ms. Zhdanova! I'm Danylo," he stuck out his hand, "I believe someone called you to arrange a meeting with me."

"Good afternoon. Yes, I spoke to Kostia. Nice to meet you."

"Nice to meet you too!"

"This is my son, Valerii," Danylo shook Valerii's hand after his mother's introduction. "You should drop the 'Ms. Zhdanova'," Ilona continued. "I don't like when people call me that except on very formal occasions. It makes me feel old." She smiled openly, and the tension between her and Danylo dissipated.

"I'm here to find out about the connections that Panchyshyn, Levchenko's competitor in the elections, has with local gangs. There are rumors that he's involved in the drug syndicate that's been active in the Kyiv and Zhytomyr regions," Danylo said.

"Ah, that's just like Levchenko, all this dirty business. I'm actually hosting a delegation from Poland and will have to leave you, but Valerii will help you with that," she said. "Call me if you need anything, here's my business card." She turned around and left the park. Her driver waited for her at the entrance. Her son and Danylo kept talking.

"Let's go to my club, I'll tell you what I know once we get there, in peace and quiet," Valerii suggested.

"Great idea, let's go!" Danylo agreed.

Valerii got into his new, pale-green Ford Mustang, and Danylo got into the car with Vova and followed him. Fifteen minutes later, they were at the club. Valerii led them around, desperate to show the place off. Planet was a large, two-story club. The building had previously been a cinema. Ilona had leveraged her connections to buy the premises for next to nothing five years before and converted them into a club. Levchenko got involved too, providing the lion's share of the needed funding. It was his gift for his son, in whose life Levchenko was otherwise never particularly invested. Danylo, Vova, and Valerii sat on a sofa, and Valerii began to tell the other two what he knew about Panchyshyn's dealings. Valerii wanted to be useful, and he wanted to make a good impression on Danylo because he knew that Danylo would relay what he learned out to Kostia, who would in turn convey it to Levchenko. Just a kid after all, Valerii wanted to mend the bridges with his dad, and he seized at the opportunity.

"I know a lot of people in Korosten. It's not a huge city, maybe 60,000 people or so, everyone knows everyone. I can tell you for sure that drug use among locals has gone up over the last year, especially among teenagers. I had to reinforce security measures here at the club – there have been more fights. Kids get here already high and aggressive and get into altercations, often physical stuff. Sometimes they bicker and fight with each other, right in the middle of the dance floor, and sometimes they nag the security guards. It's become a regular thing. I know one guy, a local dealer, who seems to have made a lot of money lately. Bought a new flat and a BMW. So I think the volume of drug sales must've gone up. He's backed by Ihor Chaplynskyi, a local oligarch. Chaplynskyi's son is the head of the Korosten police force, and Chaplynskyi also has friends in the city council who are faithful to him."

"Valerii, can you come up with some excuse to get in touch with this dealer guy you know and try to find out where he gets his drugs from?" Danylo asked.

"I think so, but I'll need time, at least a couple of days. He's out of town now and we're not close enough for me to call or text him. But he does come to my club almost every weekend, I can talk to him here. One thing I know for sure is he gets his amphetamine from somewhere else, and he gets it delivered in large batches."

"Okay, cool. One other request – can you get me the names of Chaplinskyi's friends on the city council, and find out whether they have anything to do with the Common Future NGO? We suspect that the NGO is being used for all sorts of criminal purposes."

"I'll do everything I can!"

"Thank you for your help and your hospitality. We have to get back to Kyiv now, but give me a call whenever you hear anything," Danylo said, standing up.

"No worries, I'll do my best to do it as quickly as I can. Travel safe! And come back to Planet whenever you want to, I'm always glad to see you."

On the way back to Kyiv, Danylo fell asleep in the car. It had been a long night. He woke up as they drove into Kyiv.

"What do you think about Valerii?" Vova asked. "He seems like an alright guy, yeah? Have you heard that he's Levchenko's son?"

"I don't know about all that yet, but he made a good impression. As far as I know, Levchenko doesn't really talk to him, but Valerii seems like he wants to have a relationship with his dad," Danylo said, still sleepy.

"Of course he does! Wouldn't you?"

"I can't say. I don't know what happened between them. You're only seeing one side of the situation. You think that since Levchenko has a ton of money, then Valerii should be kissing his ass to get more out of him. He could've done that ages ago but, for some reason, he hasn't. Why?" Danylo paused. "He must be plotting something and waiting for an opportune moment. I know one thing. We have to tell Kostia that Valerii is a decent guy and can be useful. Kostia will report it to Levchenko, and you and I will benefit all the more. Our boss will be pleased that he's got a son he can rely on, and Valerii will be forever grateful to us for playing a key role in restoring his relationship with his dad. I'm sure he'll be a useful ally. Get it?"

"Good thinking! You're a shrewd devil."

"Well, Vova, I don't know what's ahead of us. We need to have allies everywhere. And anyway, don't you think in the end it seems like a good cause? That'll benefit everyone involved?"

"Well, I agree," Vova said, "but listen, I'm starving. Let's go eat somewhere."

"Alright I hear you, let's do it. I'm starving too. Hardly eaten today."

The two ate heartily – *khinkali* dumplings and *chorba* stew – at a Georgian restaurant in central Kyiv, near the Olympic Stadium, and were thinking about driving back to Kotsiubynske when Danylo got a call from Kostia.

"Danylo, it's Kostia. Serhii just got in touch with me, he said Kosinchuk is on his way east. The guys are trailing him. Come meet me as soon as you can," he told Danylo, "I'll give you the paperwork you'll need to get through checkpoints in the east. You'll have to act like you're looking for a friend who used to serve in a volunteer battalion but is in the armed forces now, and you're bringing military aid you want to give to him directly. Come meet me on Malevycha Street, it's fairly central. I'll text you the exact address."

"No problem, we'll be there in five, we're just by the Olympic Stadium."

"Perfect, I'll be waiting. Hurry up!"

It took Danylo and Vova fifteen minutes of traffic violations to get to the address Kostia had given them. Two cars waited for them there, an Audi Q7 and a

Mercedes Vito. Kostia and a small team stood nearby. As Danylo stepped out of the car, Kostia invited him to join him in the Mercedes to chat.

"Danylo, here are the papers for you, Serhii, and Hrisha. The names on the papers are obviously not yours – commit them to memory, so you don't let your real names slip accidentally. Vova will wait for you in a hotel nearby, call him if you need anything. Take this bag, there's four guns in it," Kostia handed Danylo a duffle. "We've checked them all, don't worry about that. There's a bag with military uniforms, body armor, and visors in the trunk. Those are the things you're going to say you're taking to your friend, the one in the army. Keep your head on straight and be careful. Okay, time for you to go, catch up with the guys. Good luck! Just one last thing, here's a phone number. This guy's a friend. Try to get to Pisky and call him. If you need help, here's your man – and I'm sure you will..."

"Alright, thanks. We'll set off then."

Danylo and Vova set off for the east, the ATO zone. Meanwhile, Serhii and Hrisha were already on their way, following a Hyundai Tucson carrying Kosinchuk, Panchyshyn, and a third passenger that they didn't recognize. An old Ford Transit holding another two guys tailed the Tucson. Serhii and Hrisha were able to take a few pictures of the cars and their passengers before they left Irpin and followed them carefully, trying not to attract their attention. From the base in Kotsiubynske, Bot tracked Kosinchuk's car. The tracker installed on the car had enough charge to last for at least a week. The Desperados group appeared to have a firm grasp on the situation.

Danylo and Vova caught up with Serhii and Hrisha around Kharkiv. Panchyshyn and Kosinchuk drove on towards the city of Izium, the last real city before the region of Donetsk, where the ATO zone began. At almost six in the morning, they stopped for about two hours at a storage depot just outside of Izium. Meanwhile, Danylo and the rest of the Desperados crew who were along for the ride decided that Vova would stay in a hotel in Izium, where he'd lay low and await further instructions. If the team needed rescuing, that would be his role. Danylo, Serhii, and Hrisha drove on, following Panchyshyn and Kosinchuk, always hanging back by a kilometer or so. Hrisha was in the backseat, tracking Kosinchuk's car on a tablet. The guys didn't need to risk being discovered by driving any closer to Panchyshyn and his convoy. They went through a checkpoint in Izium and headed towards the city of Sloviansk, then towards Kramatorsk, before finally reaching Pokrovsk, where Panchyshyn and Kosinchuk stopped. A Mitsubishi Pajero Sport waited for them there, and the three cars continued together toward the exit from Pokrovsk, where they stopped at a shabby roadside café. The sign read: *Natali*. A bunch of guys got out of the cars and headed inside. A young man opened the doors to greet them, and carefully closed the door behind them once they all disappeared inside. He tugged on the door handle from the inside after locking the door to make sure that no one could get in and double-checked that the *Closed* sign was flipped the right way. It was 10:40am. Danylo, Serhii, and Hrisha slowly drove past the café and Hrisha took a few pictures. They pulled over on the shoulder 500 meters down the road.

Danylo looked around at the team.

"Guys, I can feel something brewing, we have to make sure we're ready for all sorts of scenarios. We have to be a step ahead of them. I have a plan that I think will make sure all our hard work doesn't go to waste."

"Yeah, go ahead. If we fail, we're dead," Serhii replied.

Hrisha was silent. His eyes were wide open, and he turned his head back and forth toward whoever was speaking.

"Serhii and I will stay here, we'll pretend we have a flat tire and we're putting a spare on. You, Hrisha, will go to the café and plant a tracking device on the Ford Transit. Just make sure no one is looking and watch out! Because if you get caught, they won't let you go easily, you know it. Got it? Everyone okay with that?" Danylo said.

"It's a bit scary, I won't lie," said Hrisha, after thinking for a few moments. "But I'll do it."

"Well, that's why I'm here, that's why you're here, and that's why Serhii's here. It will only get harder from here. You knew what you were signing up for. Don't freak out, we'll manage. Enough talking! Let's do it. Here's a phone, just dial us if anything happens, we'll know that something went wrong, and we have to get you out of there."

Hrisha got out of the car, tugged at the bill of his black baseball cap, and walked toward the café. When he reached the cars, he bent over and, fast as lighting, planted a tracking device underneath the Ford. He remained bent over, pretending to tie his laces. Suddenly, the man who worked at the café, and had greeted Panchyshyn's group when they arrived, materialized in front of Hrisha.

"Who are you? And what are you doing here?" he asked rudely.

"Well, I was visiting my relatives nearby – I'm from Kharkiv myself," Hrisha said, having tied the laces on his sneakers and slowly rising. "I just wanted a bite to eat. Are you open yet?"

"We're not! Get the hell out of here!" the guy said, taking a step forward and meaning to push Hrisha. Hrisha let out a fist and punched him in the chin, knocking him over. He hadn't known that Hrisha had once been a professional boxer.

As luck would have it, two other guys came out of the café to see what all the fuss was about.

"What's going on here?" one of them asked. He was heavy-set and wearing a military uniform.

"Good afternoon!" Hrisha replied. "I wanted to get some food at the café and this young man here started harassing me, so I punched him. I'm not looking for trouble, that's just what I was brought up to do if someone's being rude." Hrisha sounded calm and composed. Meanwhile, the man on the ground was getting his bearings. Another man – around forty, and business like in his dress and manner – stepped out of the café and approached the group outside. Hrisha thought that he must be the café's owner.

"Hey Dumpling, what the fuck happened here?" he asked the man on the ground.

"I saw this guy come over and wanted to see what he was up to, and the asshole punched me in the face!"

"I just wanted a bite to eat at the café," Hrisha retorted, "and this guy started harassing me, so I punched him, it was instinctive – how would I know what he was up to? What if he had a knife? It was pure self-defense." He spoke calmly as before.

"Dumpling, you go straight to the hospital, looks like your jaw's broken. I'll deal with you later. You, daredevil, come on in, we need a word with you."

"Demon, I'm telling you – I just wanted to do the right thing. This guy seems suspicious, he appeared out of nowhere…" the young guy protested.

"I heard you!" his boss yelled. "Go get an X-ray. Sieva, take him to the hospital," he told one of the men, then followed the other one inside, bringing Hrisha with him.

Danylo and Serhii watched down the road. They knew something was wrong.

"Hey Serhii, they got Hrisha. Why didn't he call?"

"I don't like this. I really don't like this. What are we going to do?"

"Keep your cool," Danylo said. "The most important thing is not to panic. Get the tire back on and let's wait. If nothing happens in the next hour and Hrisha doesn't come back, we'll do something. For now, the most important thing is to keep a cool head. We'll only get him – and probably ourselves – into trouble if we panic and rush."

They took Hrisha through to the café's kitchen. His phone was confiscated. A security guard was put in front of the door in case he decided to try to get out. Twenty minutes after Hrisha had been brought in, the man called Demon returned with more security guards in tow. The guards restrained Hrisha, twisting his arms behind his back.

"Well, tell us, what brought you here?" Demon asked.

"I'm from Kharkiv, was here to visit relatives."

"Guys, loosen your grip a bit. Let him stand up straight," Demon said, then kicked Hrisha twice somewhere around his liver.

Hrisha's teeth clenched with the pain, but he held firm. His regular workouts and strong abs stood him a good stead. He was tough, physically and mentally. He had known this could happen. After giving him a minute to breath, Demon took Hrisha by the face, squeezing it tight.

"I don't want to see you here anymore!" Demon shouted. "Do you understand me, you punk?"

"Yes, yes, I understand."

"Now get the fuck out of here before I change my mind!"

They gave Hrisha his phone and he walked out of the café. He had made it, miraculously, but he knew that the Desperados had been close to failure. He walked the opposite way from where Danylo and Serhii waited for him. He knew he was probably being watched. He only called Danylo once he was certain no one was trailing him.

"Hey, I'm at a bus stop, waiting for a bus to get to the Pokrovsk Railway Station. Let's meet there. I got myself into a real pickle today, will tell you all about it later. But don't worry, okay now."

"Got you. Glad to hear you're alive and well! See you soon."

Danylo and Serhii put a new license plate with a Kharkiv registration address onto their car. It was Kostia's idea, and safer that way. They drove to the railway station in Pokrovsk and parked nearby. They decided to split up. Danylo went to a coffee shop, and Serhii went to meet Hrisha at the train station. Once all three were certain no one was following them, they met up by the car and drove back towards the Natali café.

"What the hell happened to you, Hrisha?" Danylo asked as they drove.

"Well, as soon as I got the tracker onto the Ford, this guy appeared out of nowhere," Hrisha said. "He must've been high on amphetamines, by the way, judging by how agitated and aggressive he was. I punched him in the jaw and was about to run away, but two other guys came out of the café, and one thing after another… Anyway, I got kicked in the liver twice, but then they let me go."

"Thank God you're not locked up in a basement somewhere. You were so lucky! Did you see Panchyshyn or Kosinchuk? What was going on in there?" Danylo asked.

"I didn't see those two, but there was this guy everyone was calling Demon, he was in charge. At the very least I think he's in charge of things in this fucking Pokrovsk town. I also saw out of the corner of my eye that there were two other buildings behind the café. They looked like a motel and a big garage. I think Panchyshyn and Kosinchuk must be there now, sleeping."

They parked on the side of the road a couple kilometers away from the café and motel where Panchyshyn and Kosinchuk were. This was their chance to get some sleep, too. They agreed that two of them would sleep while the third one would follow the GPS trackers on Panchyshyn and Kosinchuk's cars on the tablet they had with them. They couldn't afford to miss them leaving the café. For three hours, nothing happened. Danylo stirred in his sleep. He opened one eye, then the other, and saw that Serhii – who was supposed to be monitoring the tablet – was fast asleep on his shoulder. He made a quiet wheezing sound.

"Fucking hell, wake up you loser!" Danylo shouted at Serhii.

"What happened? What?" Serhii replied through sleep, confused. Hrisha was wide awake now too, stunned and frightened.

"Look at what's happening on the screen! Are their cars still there, or did you fuck up?"

"I fucked up," Serhii managed, quietly, his heart sinking.

"Fuck! Where are they going?"

"Towards Donetsk. They're by Selydove – that's about twenty kilometers from where we are now. And I think it's just the new tracker that's moving, Panchyshyn's Tucson is still in Pokrovsk."

"Give me the tablet and let's go!" Danylo said. "Let's go to Pisky. Kostia gave me the number of someone he trusts there and told me to dial him if we have any issues. And boy do we have issues now! Think it's time to call this guy. Look, Hrisha, all your hard work is paying off. If it wasn't for what you did today, this would've been a complete fiasco and we'd be on our way back to Kyiv now, empty-handed. Your intuition is your strongest weapon."

"Definitely," Hrisha said with a wide smile. "Let's get these motherfuckers."

From their location, the drive to Pisky was only fifty-four kilometers. Danylo dialed the number Kostia had given him as soon as they started driving, but the phone had no service. Danylo, Hrisha, and Serhii were all worried, but none of them let it on. They reached Pervomaiske, another village in the Donetsk region, in about an hour, and drove into a little wood off the side of the road so that no one could spot their car. Danylo's phone remained silent: no calls or messages. Meanwhile, the Ford Transit moved across the tablet screen towards Yasynuvata. This meant that Panchyshyn and his cronies had crossed the checkpoint and entered the military zone. The Desperados group could still catch up with them in theory, but in practice it would be very difficult. They needed to cross into the territory controlled by Russian-backed separatists. There were two ways to do it. First, they could go to one of the official checkpoints, guarded by around two hundred soldiers on the Ukrainian side. Once they made it through to the other side, they'd be met by separatist forces who might have however many additional questions. Not ideal. The second option was to cross over into the occupied territories using secret hidden paths, with the help of local residents and Ukrainian soldiers fighting in the area.

Danylo, Hrisha and Serhii stayed in the car for twenty minutes. All three were silent. Danylo couldn't stand the silence and inaction, and suggested they get out and talk about what to do next.

"Going straight to those DPR jackals is a sure way to fail. And it'll have catastrophic consequences," Danylo summed up. "The only thing we can do is sit here and hope for a miracle. Even if we get caught, we'll at least get caught by Ukrainian forces, and we'll be able to come to some sort of an agreement with them."

"I say we should stay here for another couple hours and wait, then try calling the number Kostia gave you again," Serhii suggested, "If we still can't reach it, try to get in touch with Kostia himself."

"Let's do that," Danylo said. "Serhii, why don't you get bread and water from the car? I think it's time to refuel."

An hour passed, then another. Everything was quiet. Several cars drove by, but no one seemed to notice the Desperados' car hidden off the road – or at least so they thought. Four hours into their wait, a message pinged through to Danylo's phone: the phone number he'd been trying to call was back online. Danylo tried again. The phone rang, but no one picked up. Danylo was thinking that they should go back to Pokrovsk and consult Kostia regarding what to do next when suddenly, seven camouflaged men, all wearing masks and carrying AK47s, appeared from the surrounding woods and circled their car.

"Don't move! Stay where you are!" one of the men yelled.

Two others approached Danylo, Serhii, and Hrisha, searched them, and confiscated their phones and guns. Five minutes later, another two cars parked nearby. Four men stood on guard by the roadside, and another four approached the group in the woods. One of the uniformed men stepped forward.

"This is the Armed Forces of Ukraine. My alias is Johnny Blaze. Where are you from and why are you hiding here, so close to the frontline?" he asked.

"We came from Kyiv. We're bringing equipment for our friends who are fighting – armored vests and a couple visors. It's all in the trunk, you can see for yourselves," Danylo replied.

"Could it be that your friends are fighting on the occupiers' side? You look suspicious."

"We're all from the Slobozhanshyna region..." Danylo answered.

"Where exactly?"

"Kharkiv."

"Oh, if that's so, Kostia Khriashch (Gristle) says hello," Johnny Blaze said, cracking a smile. "Everything's alright, you can relax now."

The guys in camo doubled over laughing.

"You must be Danylo. Get in my car, let's talk. Guys, get used to it. It's real war over here, not what they show you on TV. We'll take you somewhere just now and then it's back to work!"

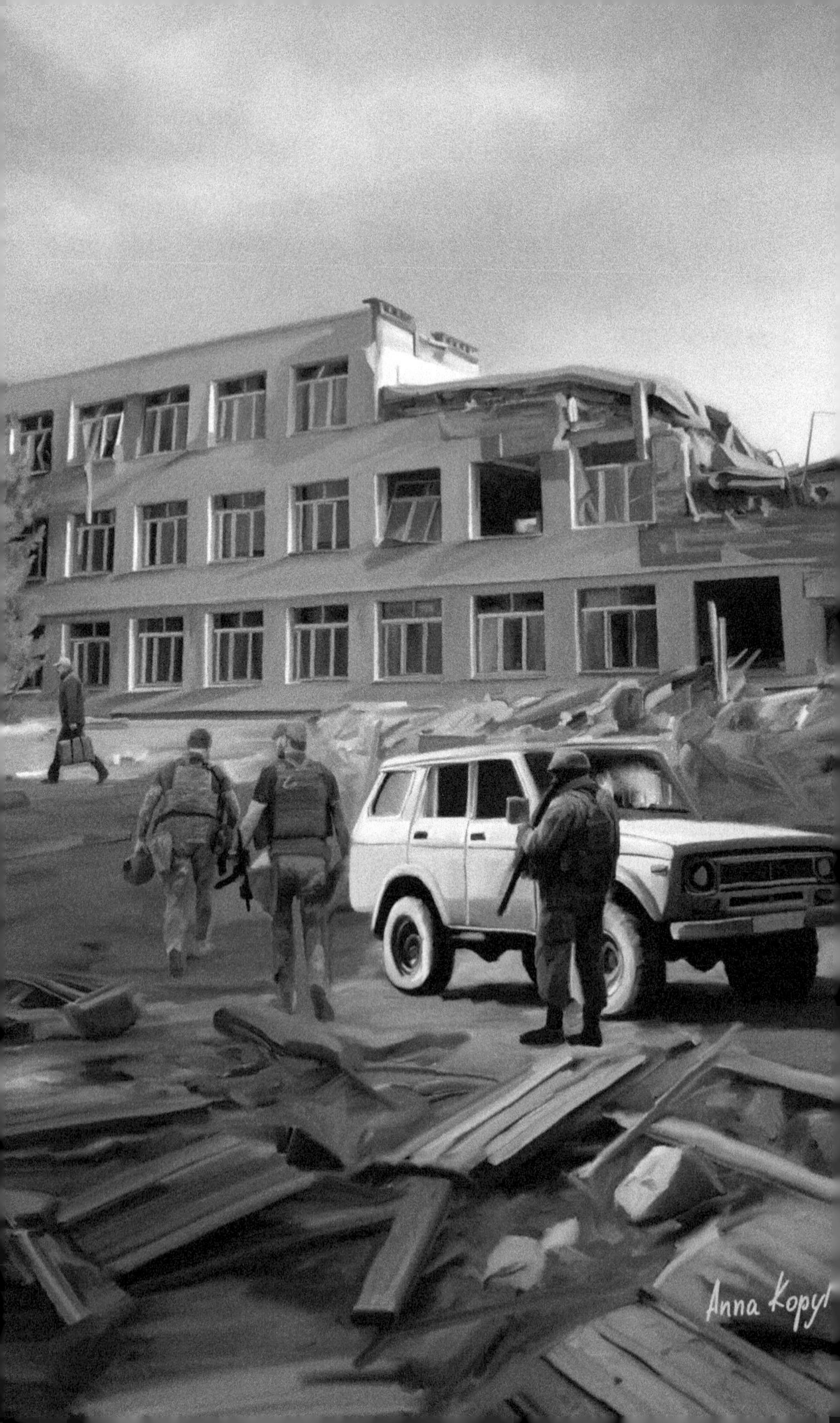
Anna Kopyl

Danylo got into an old Nissan Patrol. He felt relieved. Though he'd been surprised, he wasn't that scared. He'd prepared himself for any eventuality. Serhii and Hrisha got into their Land Cruiser and followed the Nissan. Soon the convoy approached a school building half-destroyed by pro-Russian terrorists that looked like it was functioning as a military base. Johnny Blaze and his deputy took Danylo, Serhii, and Hrisha inside and offered them tea. They politely refused. The Desperados wanted to show that their top priority was to be given instructions and to embark on their mission with as little delay as possible.

"I know you're tracking those thugs. That'll help us a lot. Can you show us where they are right now?" Jonny Blaze asked Danylo.

"We've been tracking them all the way from Irpin. Here, look," Danylo said, turning on the tablet and showing Blaze where the Ford Transit was on the map, "they're near Yasynuvata now. They haven't moved in a while."

"They're about 43, 44 kilometers away if we use the main road, but half that if we cut through the forest. We have an informer among the separatists, Mitia 'Brashka.' When Russian thugs entered Donbas, they confiscated most of his businesses, leaving him only one small facility where he makes moonshine. He contacted us himself. He can be trusted. His loyalty has been tested, more than once. We got in touch with him," Blaze said. "He'll take his van just outside Pisky, where we'll meet him. We'll pretend to be workers from his moonshine plant, and he'll get us to where we need to be. Two questions for you guys: Do you have photo and video cameras? And how are you doing in terms of physical fitness?"

Danylo exchanged looks with Serhii and Hrisha and said, "We have professional photo and video equipment. And we're pretty fit."

"I'm asking because anything can happen when we're in separatist-controlled territory. By the way, let me introduce myself properly. My name is Roman, I'm from Kolomyia in Ivano-Frankivsk. This is Zheka 'Zlatan,' he's from Dnipro – a brother-in-arms of mine and also my deputy."

Danylo, Serhii, and Hrisha introduced themselves and shook hands with the men from the unit.

"We've been here since the start of the fighting. First, we served in the Volunteer Battalion named after Ivan Sirko and then joined the Armed Forces of Ukraine. Our mutual friend Kostia has helped us a lot financially, with Levchenko's approval, as far as I understand. We had nothing, and they got us top-notch uniforms, weapons, and equipment. I just got to say that if it wasn't for volunteers like us, the Muscovite scum would've taken half of Ukraine by now. I think the volunteer movement was a decisive factor that stopped the so-called 'Russian World' from spreading across our land. People came from cities, towns, and villages all over our country to help however they could. I'll be grateful to those people for the rest of my life. The president, the government, and the parliament just watched from the distance, giving orders that didn't make any sense or even led to the deaths of our brothers-in-arms. Meanwhile, ordinary people came together and lent us a helping hand. That's why it's a matter of honor for us to catch and punish this Panchyshyn and the rest of those monsters. We won't let those scammers discredit what it means to be a volunteer in Ukraine. If they chose to profit from our country's tragedy and loss, and to profit from it in this depraved way, we have to hand out the punishment they deserve. This has nothing to do with law enforcement officials. Anyway," Roman said, his face darkening with grief and anger, "these guys are dead." It was apparent that he couldn't fathom why people like Panchyshyn and Kosinchuk would have any sort of dealings, let alone engage in drug trafficking, with separatist forces.

"Guys," Danylo said after a moment of silence, "we're also from western Ukraine – in fact from Ivano-Frankivsk – you must've guessed from our accent. But were you a fan of Wu-Tang Clan when you were a kid, Roman? Did you borrow your call sign from Clifford Smith?"

"That's right! I still listen to them. I love Wu-Tang Forever, but Method Man is my absolute favorite."

"I used to love them too," Danylo said. "I remember Gravel Pit playing at a school disco – loved that so much." Danylo's words seemed to work to resolve the tension in the room. Roman warmed to him.

"My sister and her husband live in Ivano-Frankivsk now; they have two kids. I haven't visited them in a long time..." Roman said, thinking back.

Snapping himself out of it, he clapped his hands, "Anyway, guys, enough talking, time to get to business." Everyone nodded.

"We'll go in two cars and get as close as we can to Pisky. Khotabych – an old guy who lives there and works for us – will meet us and take us into separatist-controlled territory. Four people will go. I'll go with Zlatan. Danylo, choose someone you want to go with. The rest will wait for us nearby in case of an emergency. We'll just get changed into plain clothes," Roman said. "Danylo, you and your guys look fine. Everyone take a gun with you, a couple of grenades, and photo and video equipment. When we cross over into separatist territory, we'll have to walk about five kilometers to where Mitia will be waiting for us. We'll have to do it as quickly as possible. Mitia knows people around Yasynuvata, they might be able to help us out with information on Panchyshyn's drug lab."

***

Two days after his adventures with Denys Doronin, Bot was finally able to cast aside all of his anxieties. He was dead focused on the new mission, in which he was playing a key role. He was excited and eager to succeed in the tasks he'd been given. He created a fake Instagram profile and started following Anton Trofimov's account. He liked a couple of his posts and sent him a message, to which he attached the photos of Doronin and the other man from the penthouse party. In the message, Bot told Anton that he couldn't reveal his name because he didn't want anyone to know he was gay. He said that he also felt used by the heartless Doronin and wanted to band together with Anton because of their shared distress. He wanted the photos of Doronin making out with the other man to serve as a proof of the seriousness of his intentions and urged Anton to avenge his broken heart without hesitation.

Andrii came into the room as Bot sat around at the computer; he had just sent the message to Anton and was waiting for his reply.

"What's up dude? Have you heard from Anton?"

"Not yet, he's not online."

"You better watch out or you'll get jealous yourself," Andrii said.

"Listen, if you think I don't know that you're all making fun of me behind my back, you're wrong!" Bot struck back. "Anyway, now's not the time for your stupid jokes."

Sasha came in, too. "What's all the noise about? What's the deal? What happened, Bot?"

"Oh nothing. Andrii was just telling me he's growing quite fond of Anton Trofimov," Bot decided to turn the tables.

"Shut up!" Andrii snapped back.

The situation was clear to Sasha. He told Andrii to go outside and followed him.

"Look, Andrii – I warned you, didn't I? Don't ruffle Bot's feathers with this stuff."

"You did."

"Better yet," Sasha went on, winding back his fist, "cut the joking all together." He punched Andrii straight in his chest. Andrii fell back on his ass, his face scrunched up in pain.

"What the hell? I was just kidding!" he wheezed.

"Sorry," Sasha said, shaking out his fingers.

"This is a super important time for all of us, we finally have Anton Trofimov on the hook. You've got to let Bot do his job in peace now. I hope I'm being clear now and you'll keep your mouth shut?"

"Yes, Sasha. I got it," Andrii said sharply, "but that was totally unfair."

"That was nothing. If Kostia was here, you'd have gotten it worse. Now stop whining and go back inside. Get some rest, calm down, then we'll talk."

Andrii grudgingly went inside and shut himself in one of the upstairs bedrooms. Sasha went back to Bot; he pulled up a chair next to him.

"Hey Bot, you've got news?"

"I do, actually," Bot said, "Anton read the message I just sent, but he hasn't replied yet."

"Oh, great! Now we just have to wait. And one other thing," he said, nudging Bot, "keep what just happened under the rug and go make peace with Andrii. We don't need this infighting. Got it?"

"Got it, yes. I don't have to be told more than once."

"Sweet. I'm leaving for a couple of hours on business, but let me know if anything happens." Sasha didn't really have any business in Kyiv, he just thought maybe a massage would get rid of some of the tension he felt accumulating in his body.

Bot remained in front of his computer screen, unfazed. He saw that Anton had called Doronin twice but had received no answer. Bot checked when Anton made the calls and saw that it was almost right after he read the message Bot had sent him on Instagram. He figured that shit was about to hit the fan and called Sasha.

"Sasha, Anton's calling Denys, but he's not replying yet."

"Hey, got it," Sasha replied. "Don't get involved yet, just keep an eye on what happens next."

"That's the plan. We should give them a chance to get into it with each other."

"Good idea. Then we'll get involved and offer Anton a vision of revenge he probably won't be able to resist, with emotions running that high…"

An hour later, Anton tried calling Doronin one last time, but in vain, and then forwarded the photos Bot had sent him, writing, "You will regret this."

Bot was tired of waiting around and fell asleep in front of his screen. When he woke up and saw what was happening, he yelled to the others, "Guys, Anton has amped up the stakes!"

Andrii heard the yelling and came into the room. "What happened, Bot?"

"Game on. Anton sent Denys the photos I sent him! Oh, and by the way, Andrii," he stuck his hand out, "let's just shake hands and put today behind us. Sorry, didn't mean for things to go that far."

"I'm sorry too, Bot. All good, let's move on. Did Denys respond?"

"Not yet, but he saw the message almost as soon as Anton sent it. He must be shocked. Can you call Tarnavskyi and tell him that shit's hit the fan and we need him here?"

"No problem, calling him now."

Half an hour later, Sasha was back at Kotsiubynske. Bot gave him the rundown of what had happened while he was gone, and Sasha smiled with glee.

"Alright, guys, those two have taken our bait! Did Denys reply to Anton?"

"Yeah, he just did: 'Don't do anything stupid, I can explain.'"

"Time to make a move. Why don't you message Anton something like: 'I hope you won't ignore Doronin's nasty move and will pay him back in kind. I can help you with that if you want.' What do you think, is that okay? I'm not great when it comes to love affairs."

"I would add: 'I'll be waiting for your reply,'" Andrii said.

"Look at you pair of writers. You've messed around with a few girls I bet, and now you're suddenly so demure," Bot said, smirking at Sasha and Andrii. He sent the message to Anton.

Less than ten minutes later, Anton replied. The message read, "Thanks, I really am grateful. What do you suggest?"

"We don't have time to reinvent the wheel," Sasha said, springing into action, "so let's start with what it is that we need to achieve. We have to get them together at some apartment or hotel and get some footage of them, right? So, we have to get Anton to do what we want him to do. Come on, guys, fucking help me out here! Why suddenly so quiet? What do you think?"

"I think we should make use of the fact that Anton's ego's been wounded. He thinks he's so impossibly cool and that everyone owes him… But look at him now, being thrown away like a piece of trash," Bot said, stroking his chin.

"Keep going," Sasha replied.

"I think we should play to his lustful side. Let's say something like this: 'Make him regret his decision; make him submit to you; make him do whatever you want him to do, because now you have power over him.'"

"Bot," Sasha said, looking excited, "you're a genius at manipulation. Send it now!"

"Alright, I'll send it. Wait – hold on! Most importantly, we have to come up with a plan that Anton can carry out, and then offer it to Anton. We'll figure it out from there and finish the mission."

"Right, but send him your message anyway – it'll just be the bait," Sasha said. "He'll get all wound up, and meanwhile we'll come up with a plan he'll want to follow. I think he's dead eager on bringing Doronin to book and getting some self-esteem back, which Doronin crushed."

They were all quiet for a moment, imagining different scenarios for how things might unfold. Bot broke the silence.

"Guys, Doronin's boyfriend arrives from Sweden tomorrow. He just messaged Doronin, asking whether he'd be able to meet him at the airport. Doronin replied: 'Sure, what time? I missed you!'"

"Come on, Bot, we don't need the details." Sasha said.

"Fine, I'm just telling you what's happening. Also, Ludvig Blomquist's arrival is a trump card for us, and we have to play it well."

"Here's what I propose," Sasha began. "Let's tell Anton when Ludvig arrives from Stockholm to make sure he trusts us. We'll encourage him to go to the airport when Doronin will be there to meet his boyfriend and blackmail him until he agrees to do whatever Anton wants, to avoid being humiliated in front of his boyfriend. We also somehow have to get the idea of spending one last night with Doronin into Anton's head. We'll have to suggest that possibility to him… Hey Bot, why don't you put all this into a message to Anton, and then we'll wrap up for today and wait for his reply. Let's not overdo it. Does anyone have any objections or concerns?"

"All sounds good to me," Andrii said.

"I'm on board too," Bot chimed in. "But another interesting development: Ludvig just texted Doronin telling him he's off to an IT conference in Lviv on Tuesday and will be back to Kyiv on Thursday night."

"Okay guys, we don't need to tell this to Anton yet, but when the time comes, we'll be able to take advantage of this," Sasha said. "You guys stay here in Kotsiubynske, and I'll meet with Kostia in town. I'll tell him what we've been up to today. If something urgent comes up, just call. I'll leave you cash too so you two can order some food, the fridge is empty."

He got into a car and drove to the Brooklyn bar, where he was meeting Kostia. After the two talked about the latest developments concerning Anton Trofimov and Sasha was on his way out, he ran into Danylo's ex, Diana, at the entrance.

"Hi Sasha," she said. "Haven't seen you in ages. You're in Kyiv now?"

"Hey Diana! I wasn't expecting to run into you here. I'm just here for a couple of days for work. What about you? What are you up to?"

"I'm doing great, it's my second year in Kyiv. I'm a journalist now," she said, "working for one of the TV channels here. How's Danylo doing? Are you still in touch with him?"

"Yes, we're still friends. I actually just saw him recently. He was also in town, and we met up here."

"Tell him I say hello if you see him again. It's nice to see you again too, but I've got to run, I'm late to a date with my friends," Diana blushed and looked a bit embarrassed after talking about Danylo.

"Nice to see you too! I'll tell him you said hello. Have a nice evening!" Sasha noticed Diana's sheepishness when it came to Danylo. He smiled. He got into his car and drove towards the Pechersk flat. He got McDonald's on his way there and called his wife to tell her he was doing alright and to ask her to give their kids a big hug from him. By the time he got to the flat, it was past eleven. He rolled a joint, stretched out on the sofa, and started replaying the events of the past few days in his head. His unexpected meeting with Diana made him think about his time as a student, when he, Danylo, and Diana went to the Carpathians for a holiday, and he got so drunk that he broke down a door. His now wife, then just a girl he liked, was there too. She and her friends couldn't calm him down; he was entirely out of it. Before he fell asleep, his thoughts once again returned to Danylo, and how Diana had reappeared under such unexpected circumstances, and how odd it was that she was living and working in Kyiv. A strange turn of events, he thought.

Sasha was back at the Kotsiubytnske base by seven the next morning. Bot and Andrii had just woken up and were showering, each in their own bathroom, when he arrived. He made coffee for everyone and waited for them in the kitchen. Fifteen minutes later, the team was ready for action.

"Morning guys!" Sasha said. "What you got, Bot? Has Anton replied?"

"Morning Sasha. Yes, he has. He also tried to video-call me, but I didn't pick up."

"That's good. Let's limit our interactions to messages and not meet him in person – at least for now. What did he say in his message?"

"He said he was grateful for my help and that he owes me a bottle of whisky. He also said he'll pay Doronin back for what he did."

"What does that mean?" Sasha asked.

"I don't know yet," Bot said.

"Okay. Message him this: 'What are you going to do? Intercept Doronin in the airport before he meets Ludvig, or confront both of them when they're leaving the airport?'"

"Alright, just a sec," Bot said, typing. "But do we need him thinking about something so dramatic?"

"Well, whether we're the ones putting the ideas into his head or not, we need to know what he's going to do," Sasha said.

"I just don't understand what we can achieve by pushing him on this course of action."

"Look, I'm the one responsible for the outcome of this mission, so just do what I say!" Sasha shot back.

"Come on Bot, don't show off," Andrii said, making a show of backing up Sasha. "We all know you're a smart guy, but Sasha's got it right, here."

"Cool off, fine. Was just expressing my opinion. Look, I sent the message you wanted me to send," Bot said.

"Great, now we wait. When does Ludvig's flight arrive?" Sasha asked.

"Eight Kyiv time," Bot muttered.

"Then we have ten to twelve hours before the mission hits its final stretch, so get your shit together and focus. Now is not the time to sulk and act all offended. That goes for both of you! I hope we won't have to return to this conversation again. Now let's get to work!" Sasha ordered and left the room.

He was on the verge of a nervous breakdown. On one hand, his wife kept nagging him to come back home, saying that his work trip wasn't going to end well. On the other hand, he felt the weight of the Trofimov mission, the responsibility on his shoulders for its success, that he owed to his boss Kostia and his boss's boss, Levchenko. Over the past week or so,

Sasha had lost weight and picked up smoking cigarettes again. He'd already been smoking plenty of weed; it helped him calm down and relax when he was feeling wound up. He decided to go for a walk around the grounds of the house to relax a bit. He even turned his phone off in an effort to switch off completely. He lit a cigarette, took a puff, and behind him heard Andrii yell his name. He turned to see Andrii step out of the house, striding quickly toward him.

"I'm here," Sasha yelled back. He put out his cigarette and walked in Andrii's direction.

"Something's wrong with your phone? I couldn't reach you," Andrii said.

"Maybe there's no service back there. What happened?"

"Anton replied, he's asking for advice, what he should do."

"Alright, let's go get Bot." Sasha turned and walked back toward the house.

Moments later, the three were back together again.

"Well, Bot, game on. Buckle in, boys," Sasha said, gleeful.

"Anton's online, must be waiting for our reply," Bot reported. "What should we do?"

"Okay, here's what you should tell him: 'Don't lose your cool. You already hold all the aces. The photos I sent you will get you, at the very least, a night of full control over Doronin. You'll be able to tell him what you think about him, and anything else you might want to tell him… You can drop it on him at the Boryspil Airport when he gets there to meet his darling Swedish boyfriend. Remember, his plane gets in at eight tonight.'"

"Woah, very good!" Bot said with a wicked smile. He sent the message.

"You're a real expert at this stuff," Andrii said, always ingratiating himself.

"Let's see what comes out of it. Hopefully it gets him headed in the direction that we need. Meanwhile, Andrii, why don't you get the car from the garage – I think it was one of Levchenko's lovers' cars – and go to Doronin's house? Keep an eye on him throughout the day."

"Cool, I'm gone. Should I plant a tracker on Doronin's car?"

"Good thinking. Where are our GPS trackers, Bot?" Sasha asked.

"I'll get them. I got all that stuff in my room," Bot said, "was just checking if everything was working alright."

Soon Andrii left, and Sasha and Bot stayed together at the Kotsiubynske base, in front of the screen, eager to see how Anton Trofimov would reply to their message. Their wait wasn't long.

"Sasha!" Bot called out, "Anton just wrote back. He says: 'I don't know what I'd do without you! Whoever you are, I owe you big time. Thanks again.' I'll just say: 'Mr. Justice.' Short and sweet."

"Sure, why not. Just make sure he won't chicken out. He has to meet Doronin at the airport. He has to – I want this weight off my shoulders."

"No problem, will text him now."

"You want more coffee?" Sasha asked, changing the topic.

"Sure, thanks. Oh," Bot said drawing it out, "Anton just wrote that he can't wait to see the fear in Doronin's eyes tonight at the airport."

"High five, Bot! He took the bait, he's in it now. Now we just have to make sure he carries out the rest of the plan," Sasha said. "I got another idea. Why don't you call Doronin and say you haven't seen or heard from him since the party and were wondering how he is doing? And ask him what his plans are for the rest of the day…"

"You don't think he thinks that I took the photos and sent them to Anton?"

"I think if you suddenly disappear, then he might, but not if you call him first and say how grateful you are he dragged you out of the house on Friday night to such a great party. And don't forget to mention that you wouldn't mind doing it all again."

"You're right," Bot said, "it should be impossible to link me to Anton Trofimov, which should lead him to conclude that it was one of his close friends that sent the photos to Anton. Zhenia Karavaiev and Fedia Berlin are probably the two most obvious suspects."

"Yes. And your hands are as clean as a mountain spring in the Carpathians," Sasha said.

The two pulled their chairs up to the table and sipped at their coffee. Bot rang Doronin.

"Hey Denys! How have you been since Friday? Sorry I didn't call you sooner," Bot side-eyed Sasha, "took me a while to recover. We really went hard, didn't we?"

"Hi. Yeah, I felt awful," Doronin said on the other end of the line, "but I'm fine now. I'm getting old. Used to be able to stay out for three nights in a row, and now it takes me a whole day to recover from just one."

"What are you up to today? Want to meet up tonight for a walk and dinner? I'm kind of getting bored here on my own."

"I'm just hanging out around home now, but I have plans this evening, so won't be able to meet. Sorry!"

"That's alright, another time then."

"I just wanted to ask you," Doronin said, pausing. "I'm having trouble with something and was wondering if you could help."

"Sure, no problem! Let me know when you want to meet and we can talk about it."

"Thanks! I'll call you tomorrow afternoon and we can figure it out. Have a good day!"

"You too." Bot hung up.

"What did he say at the end there?" Sasha asked, only having heard Bot's side of the conversation.

"He said he needs help with something," Bot said.

"That's good news. If he thought you were implicated in all this misfortune, he'd avoid you. I think I have another idea, but it can wait."

***

Doronin hadn't left his flat for two days other than to get more booze from the nearest grocery store. Since Anton Trofimov had sent him photos from the party, he'd been in the grips of panic. Briefly, the weight of his paranoia had made him consider suicide. Cocaine and whiskey – supplied by Fedia Berlin – were in no small part responsible for his state of mind. Doronin knew that the photos could destroy his reputation, his career, and his relationship with Ludvig. There was an image he couldn't get out of his head: one sunny spring morning the country wakes up to a bombshell news article about a university professor's promiscuous lifestyle. The article would of course be accompanied by photographic evidence: Doronin making out with a guy with his pants off. The possibility gripped him with fear. He sat around at home, coming up with dozens of ways to get out of that situation – some of them fairly radical. His despair was pushing him toward dangerous, even fatal actions, but so far, his common sense had prevailed. What preoccupied him most was the question of who gave the photos to Anton.

Sasha and Bot, pleased with the fruits of their labor, got ready for the evening ahead. Sasha tried to stay positive and keep his doubt and fear at bay. Bot was anxious too. He thought that Anton was a coward and it was possible that he'd bail out of the airport confrontation with Doronin at the last minute.

Just before six that evening, Sasha's phone rang with a call from Andrii.

"Doronin is leaving the house," Andrii said. "I'm tracking his car and will follow not far behind."

"Great. Maintain a good distance," Sasha said." Let us know if he changes course on his way to Boryspil. Text is fine."

Sasha and Bot set out for the Boryspil Airport a few minutes later.

***

Doronin stopped by a grocery store to pick up some seafood and a bottle of white wine for dinner. He got to the airport early; there was hardly any traffic leaving Kyiv on Sunday night. Sasha, Bot, and Andrii weren't far behind. Doronin ordered a latte in an airport café and, like the others, was visibly anxious as he waited for the Stockholm flight to land. Andrii was also in the airport building, keeping a watchful eye on Doronin, while Sasha and Bot remained in their car. They hadn't heard from Anton Trofimov, and Andrii hadn't seen him in the airport, either. Their anxiety slowly ramped up as it seemed more and more likely that he just wouldn't show. Just after seven thirty, Doronin finished his coffee and headed toward the arrival hall where he would meet his boyfriend. According to the arrivals screen, the Stockholm flight was expected to land on time. Just as the prospect of seeing Ludvig was beginning to somewhat ease the tension that tightened Doronin's body, he heard a woman's voice behind him, through the noise and bustle of the airport.

"Good evening, Mr. Doronin! How are you? You don't look that great. Maybe you don't recognize me?"

Doronin, turning, felt at a loss for words but managed to squeeze out, "Of course I do. You're Liza Trofimova."

"Yes. This will make our conversation easier and help us clear up the situation that's like the Sword of Damocles hanging over your head." Liza looked elegant, as always, and the trace of her perfume followed her through the airport hall.

"I don't know what you're talking about."

"Let me explain. I have your fate in my hands. Either stop acting like you don't know what I'm talking about, and we can discuss your options; or the photos from Friday's party will be on the principal's desk, and all over the internet, tomorrow. Remember, we're in Kyiv: not in Stockholm or in New York. Your sexual preferences will be greeted with a lot less understanding here. Do you understand me now?"

"What do you want from me?" Doronin's voice shook.

"I want my brother to be happy. Do what he says, and I'll leave you alone. Bye!" She smiled sweetly, turned around, and walked gracefully to the nearest exit.

Doronin stood very still. He hadn't expected the blackmail and the retribution to come so soon. That Liza Trofimova knew he would be in Boryspil at that very moment sent him into a full-blown panic, a kind he had never experienced before.

Andrii stood just a couple meters away and watched closely as the scene unfolded. He recognized Liza Trofimova and texted Sasha that Anton sent his sister in his place. Sasha was as shocked by this as Andrii and Bot. What was unfolding was beginning to deviate from their plan, and Liza's appearance only further complicated the situation.

The three guys drove back to Kotsiubynske.

Doronin met Ludvig and they went back to Doronin's flat, where he cooked a dinner for his boyfriend.

It was quiet at the Kotsiubynske base, even with the team back. They decided it was too early to tell anything to Kostia as they were still unsure of how to proceed. They knew their next move would have to be decisive. Sasha sat at the table thinking; his eyes were focused on one point, and he nervously fidgeted with a pen. Andrii tried not to think too deeply about their situation, rationalizing to himself that it wasn't his responsibility to come up with the plan, that's not what he was paid to do. He flicked through photos of girls on

Instagram on his phone. Bot monitored Doronin's text messages on his computer.

Sasha's phone rang. It was Kostia.

"Hey Sasha," Kostia said, "What's up? Everything alright with you guys? Haven't heard from you today."

"We just got back to Kotsiubynske," Sasha replied, glancing over at Bot and Andrii.

"Well, how are things?"

"Anton's sister Liza showed up to confront Doronin at the airport instead of Anton himself, so we're kind of scratching our heads about what to do now. We just didn't expect it."

"Come on, don't be discouraged! You have to expect anything from that family. To be honest, it doesn't surprise me," Kostia said, "they're fucking scammers. The most important thing for you now is to not get caught. Otherwise, continue doing what you're doing, see how the situation unfolds, improvise. You're good at it! And keep me posted about what's going on, call me whenever. For now, I think you can sit back and wait to see what happens, because something will certainly happen. Right, I got to go, speak soon! And keep your spirits up, everything will be alright."

The guys did as Kostia said, and the night went by, uneventful. The next day, they decided to lay low and not rush things. They would wait for Doronin to call Bot and take it from there. Tension was high and each of the three constantly ran through possible scenarios in their head. The fear of the unknown kept their adrenaline levels high. Bot got a phone call just before four in the afternoon.

He picked up, and Doronin spoke on the other end. "Hi," he said anxiously, "are you free to meet later today?"

"Hi! Sure, just let me know when and where," Bot said, sounding calm and confident. "And let's make it after six if that's okay, I still got some work I need to finish."

"How's 7:30pm by the fountain in the Holosiivskyi Park? Have you been there before, do you know where it is?"

"I haven't but don't worry, Google will help me," Bot said.

"Great, see you there then!"

"See you soon."

As Bot hung up, Sasha was already ringing Kostia. When he got through, he told him about Bot's meeting with Doronin. They figured that the meeting was to their advantage and would help them to steer the situation in their favor. Given that Doronin was in despair and was obviously looking for support and advice, he would easily fall prey to their plot. At least so they thought.

Sasha, Andrii, and Bot arrived at the Holosiivskyi Park just after seven, in separate cars. At 7:30pm, Bot waited in front of the fountain. Sasha and Andrii were nearby in case of an emergency. Doronin was a few minutes late. He walked fast and appeared very agitated.

"You don't look great," Bot said as they shook hands. "Is everything okay?"

"Let's go for a walk. I'll try to explain it to you," Doronin said.

"Okay, lead the way!" Bot replied, and the two set off.

"I'll start by saying that some recent events have made me distrustful of anyone I used to be close with. You're the only person I can tell this to," Doronin started.

Bot's stomach churned as he listened, but he managed not to lose composure. "I'm all ears. Rest assured, I don't have anyone to tell anything to. I know how to keep secrets, and," he emphasized, "I don't know anyone in Kyiv."

"Look, I'm gay. I hope you're okay with that," Doronin said.

"Well, if you expect me to say I'm gay, too, I won't."

"No, no, not at all! That's not what I was trying to say – sorry, it's my nerves."

"Of course I'm okay with that. I think everyone can decide for themselves who to love," Bot responded.

"You know, I knew you were a good, fair person from the moment I met you. That's why I'm turning to you now. I'm in a lot of trouble after Friday's party. It can put an end to my career and ruin my relationship with someone I love. I think I might be in danger of physical violence, too."

"What the hell! What on earth have you done?" Bot did his best to look bewildered.

"A friend of mine gave me a blow job at that afterparty we went to, someone got it on camera, and now I'm being blackmailed with those photos. They're threatening to show the photos to my boyfriend Ludvig and the university principal."

"Holy shit, I don't know what to say. That's big city life for you!" Bot said. "Give me a moment to catch my breath, I'm not used to things like that.

"Okay. Tell me more about Ludvig," he went on. "Also where did the violence bit come from?"

"Ludvig is my boyfriend. We live together. We're hoping to move abroad and get married in the next six months or so. Violence – well, I think that the people who are blackmailing me – a student of mine whose feelings I neglected and his sister – are capable of getting someone to harm me. They must've hired a private detective or bribed someone I know to get those photos. Their dad is a big deal in one of the ministries, so money and connections aren't an issue for them."

"Woah Denys, you're in a real pickle. But maybe it isn't hopeless."

"I'd like to believe you…"

"How can I be useful?" Bot asked.

"The name of the student who's blackmailing me is Anton. I don't know what he wants from me yet, but I suspect he might try to get me to sleep with him to soothe his ego, and then he'll leave me alone. At least that's what I'm hoping for," Doronin said.

"And you'd do that?"

"I don't have a choice. I think he'll probably let me know what he wants from me tonight or tomorrow."

"Call me as soon as you hear from him," Bot told Doronin. "You can count on me. I'll be there for you."

After the meeting, Bot came to realize the scale of what the Desperados group and his own actions had dragged Doronin into. As he told Sasha about his conversation with Doronin on their way back to Kotsiubynske, he felt more and more ill at ease. Kostia and his bodyguards arrived to Kotsiubynske an hour and a half later, and Bot had to relive his conversation with Doronin once again. He kicked himself for agreeing to this job instead of staying in Ivano-Frankivsk, making decent money, and living a normal life. Instead, tempted by a couple thousand bucks, he was now responsible for ruining people's lives. Until he joined the Desperados group, Bot had been a normal IT worker. Not a saint – he loved getting drunk with his friends and had frequented local brothels. But he'd never been involved in anything like what he was doing in Kyiv. It was his friends Serhii and Hrisha who'd recommended Bot to Sasha Tarnavskyi when they learned he was looking for a hacker. Bot had known them since they were all kids, growing up in the same apartment block. They'd gone through a lot together; they knew Bot could be trusted.

***

When Doronin got back home, Ludvig was still at work, getting ready for his Lviv conference the next day. He was travelling to Lviv in the morning and would come back in a couple of days. Doronin wanted to iron out the situation with Anton Trofimov before his return. He resigned himself to the fate that had befallen and decided that his goal was to do everything within his power to save his relationship with Ludvig. He had three days to make it happen. He also thought he could get Ludvig to help find Bot a job at a European or US-based IT firm to thank Bot for his help and support in the delicate matter. He even came up with a story that would make Ludvig unlikely to say no to his talented and promising IT friend. Having weighed all the pros and cons, Doronin decided he wouldn't sit around waiting. He did a line of cocaine, downed a glass of whiskey, and called Anton Trofimov.

"Hi Anton. We need to talk and resolve this misunderstanding as adults, as civilized people," Doronin said. His voice sounded a touch nervous but full of resolve.

"Oh hello. We do or you do?"

Doronin paused, took a breath, and regained control.

"Look, let's meet in person and talk about things. We're not strangers, after all. Enough of this shit. Stop messing with me."

"Honey, I haven't even started. I can tell you're nervous. I wonder how your precious boyfriend will react when he finds out that as soon as he leaves Kyiv, you're out there looking for cheap thrills with other guys."

"What about tomorrow night?" Doronin said, ignoring Anton's threat.

"I can't tomorrow," Trofimov said flatly. "How about the weekend? Though I'm sorry, I forgot, you must be busy on the weekend with your California dreaming."

"You're right, actually. I'm having a romantic dinner with Ludvig, and then we're going to get into a hot tub together, and then we'll have sex. I can't wait for him to fuck me," Doronin went all-in, feeling the whisky and cocaine. "Meanwhile you'll probably be jerking off to the photos you're blackmailing me with. So Wednesday night? Or I hang up." He knew his risky behavior was likely to pay off – Anton Trofimov was turned on by being treated like dirt.

"You're playing with fire. Be careful – you might just get yourself into even more trouble. Wednesday works. I'll call you tomorrow and let you know where and when. Sweet dreams."

"Good night," Doronin hung up, threw his phone on the table, and yelled, "Fucking asshole!"

He couldn't sleep that night. He had two and a half days to get it all over with, and the thoughts circling in his head wouldn't let him relax. Ludvig noticed his nerves and anxiety and tried asking what was wrong, but Doronin would change the subject or complain about his work. Ludvig left for the airport early in the morning, and Doronin called Bot as soon as he was out of the apartment. It was barely seven.

"Good morning, did I wake you up?"

"Morning! No, all good, I just woke up anyway. Everything alright?" Bot asked.

"Can't tell you on the phone, I think it might be tapped. Those bastards are capable of anything. Let's meet in the gym parking lot tonight, say nine?"

"No problem. See you then. Everything will be alright, Denys, hold on tight."

"Thank you," Doronin said, rubbing his head. "I'm so grateful for your support."

"It's nothing, you're welcome." Bot hung up. His stomach churned as he struggled to come to terms with the cruelty of what was happening, but there was no turning back.

***

Sasha and Andrii pulled into the gym around eight thirty. Sasha stayed in the car and Andrii stepped out for a little surveillance loop to make sure that no one suspicious was hovering around. He walked back to the car convinced that the scene was quiet. Bot arrived at the parking lot a few minutes before nine, and Doronin not long after. Bot was visibly nervous. Sasha had asked him to wear a wire so that he could hear the entire conversation between Bot and Doronin himself and record it for Kostia.

Bot walked up to Doronin's car, praying for the whole ordeal to be over as quickly as possible. He knocked on his window and got into the passenger seat.

"How are you? Tell me what happened!"

"Couldn't be worse. Feels like the world is about to end," Doronin said. "Anton called this afternoon and said he'll be waiting for me tomorrow at the Good Time spa resort in Tolokun."

"And you agreed?"

"I had to. I had no choice. I have no time. I need to figure this shit out by Thursday."

"Okay, got you. How can I help?" Bot asked, genuinely.

"Look, I want to have options if things get really dire, if Anton and I fail to reach an agreement and he and his family continue blackmailing me. I need you to come with me and plant a camera in our room while Anton and I are having dinner. I'm just a university professor, and he's the son of a deputy minister, and maybe a video of us having sex will be threatening enough for them to get off my back – at least for a while. That'll buy me the time I need to finish my paperwork to move to the US with Ludvig. I promise I'll help you find a job at a top IT firm abroad in exchange for your help. What do you think, are you in?" Doronin finally asked.

"To be honest, I'm kind of shocked. I didn't expect anything like that. They've got you in a corner," Bot said. "But I'm in. I'll do whatever you need me to do to help you get out of this shit. What's our action plan?"

"An old friend of mine owns a detective agency," Doronin replied. "He'll bring me a mini camera tomorrow and show me how to use it. I told him I need it for a colleague of mine who thinks his wife is cheating on him. I'll call in sick at work, so I can meet you in the afternoon to figure out the camera. We'll go to Tolokun around seven tomorrow night, in separate cars of course. It's about sixty kilometers outside of Kyiv. I'll go to the restroom at some point during the dinner and give you the keys to our room, and you can get in and plant the camera. That's how I see it all happening, at least. What do you think, is it a stupid plan?"

"No, makes sense to me. I'll call this spa resort tomorrow morning and book a table for myself at their restaurant, just in case."

"Good idea! I have no words to say how grateful I am for everything you're doing for me. I will never forget it. Thank you so, so much!" said Doronin.

"Forget about it. Anyone would do the same. Okay, I've got to go now, I have an early start tomorrow. I'll come over to yours around two. Good night!" Bot said, leaving.

"Good night. Thanks again," Doronin waved as the two parted.

Sasha couldn't have been happier about what he heard. Things were falling into place. Doronin all but gave them exactly what they wanted on a silver platter. That night, the guys met up with Kostia at the Kotsiubynske base. Kostia praised their work and handed out a cash bonus, a thousand bucks each. But not all of them were happy about it. Bot was uneasy, railed by an anxiety that only kept growing since meeting with Doronin. He wanted to run away as far as he could from Kotsiubynske and the rest of the Desperados team; the only thing holding him back was the hope that he might yet be able to help Doronin. Bot felt that he had to find Doronin a way out of this terrible trap, or else the guilt would eat him up from the inside.

The next day, Bot went over to Doronin's flat in the afternoon to test the camera and then met up with him again later that night, around 7:30pm, at a gas station in the village of Stari Petrivtsi, forty minutes outside of Kyiv. From there, they headed to the Good Time spa resort in Tolokun. Sasha and Andrii, as always, were close by, waiting to see how the evening unfolded. Doronin was the first to arrive at the resort, which was located on a scenic riverbank. He entered and went straight up to the room where Anton Trofimov was already waiting for him. Fifteen minutes later, Bot was at the resort's restaurant. He pretended to skim through the menu as he waited for Doronin and Trofimov to appear in the dining room. They didn't come down until around nine. Doronin looked annoyed but focused; he didn't look like someone who was enjoying himself. Anton Trofimov was the opposite – he talked constantly and made silly jokes. He was drunk and had taken a few lines of coke before the dinner.

"What do you think about the coke, Denys? My dealer said it's the cleanest you can get in Kyiv these days, and he knows what he's talking about," Anton said with a stupid grin.

"Yes, it's obviously top notch. My gums went immediately went numb," Doronin replied coldly.

"By the way, Lisa says hello. Isn't she an angel?"

"She just needs a halo. Can you tell me something? Who took those pictures of me at the penthouse party? And how did you find out when I would be at the airport? Is this your sister's work?"

"No, she has nothing to do with it. She's too busy for this sort of stuff. There are people out there whose love for you seems no less than mine."

"I don't get it. Care to explain?" Doronin asked.

"Oh, so you want me to tell you everything, don't you? You really think I'm that stupid? Why don't you think about it yourself," Anton shot back.

"To be honest, I couldn't imagine you'd turn out to be so rotten inside," said Doronin, standing up. "One minute, I need to use the restroom."

"Well come on, hurry up," Anton said.

Doronin walked quickly to the restroom. Bot followed him inside, and Doronin gave him the key to his and Trofimov's hotel room. They agreed to meet again in the bathroom an hour later. Bot was supposed to text Doronin an "Ok" first. Bot rushed to the room as fast as he could. He opened the door, walked in, and attached the camera to a curtain rod so that it could capture the entire room. He then calmly walked back to the restaurant. His Caesar salad arrived as he sat down. He pulled out his laptop and checked that the camera was recording. Everything seemed to be working fine. An hour later, Bot discretely handed the key back to Doronin. Meanwhile, Doronin and Trofimov finished a bottle of whisky. The tension between them was only more palpable now. They went up to their room. Bot went back to his car and texted Sasha that everything was going according to plan. Bot had the laptop broadcasting the footage from the camera on the seat next to him; he didn't want to look. In an effort to escape the reality of what was happening, Bot put his headphones in, turned on classical music, and closed his eyes. He nodded off for an hour or so and woke up to his phone ringing. Bot picked up.

"Fuck, this is it, this is the end," Doronin repeated franticly.

"What happened?"

"What sins am I being punished for? God help me!"

"Okay. You have to calm down and tell me what happened," Bot said. He rested the laptop on his knees and saw Doronin in the middle of the room. Anton Trofimov lay next to him, unmoving.

"Anton isn't breathing, I can't feel his pulse, but I'm not a doctor, I have no idea what to do! We were wrestling just a few moments ago, he wanted to punch me in the face but missed, I pushed him, and he fell and hit his head on the corner of the stone fireplace."

"Try to stay calm and don't leave the room. I'll be up there in a couple of minutes. Did you hear me?" Bot was shouting.

"Yes." Doronin said weakly.

"The most important thing is to stay where you are!"

Bot called Sasha as soon as he hung up on Doronin. "We have an issue. A complete nightmare. Where are you? You have to come here as quickly as you can!"

"We're just a few kilometers away, we'll be there in ten. Tell me what happened," Sasha ordered.

"Not on the phone, no. I'll wait for you just outside of the resort parking lot – I'll leave the car here. Just don't ask anything now, I'll explain everything when I see you."

Some ten minutes later, Bot was in the car with Sasha and Andrii. His voice was shaky, but he explained what had just happened. Sasha got out of the car and dialed Kostia. His hands shook. Bot and Andrii didn't say anything. The silence in the car was complete. Kostia told Sasha to get the camera out of Doronin and Trofimov's hotel room and get the fuck out of there. Bot tried calling Doronin, but all he heard was: "The person you are trying to call cannot take your call now. Please try again later."

Part 2.

Reykjavík:

The secret of the Atlantic

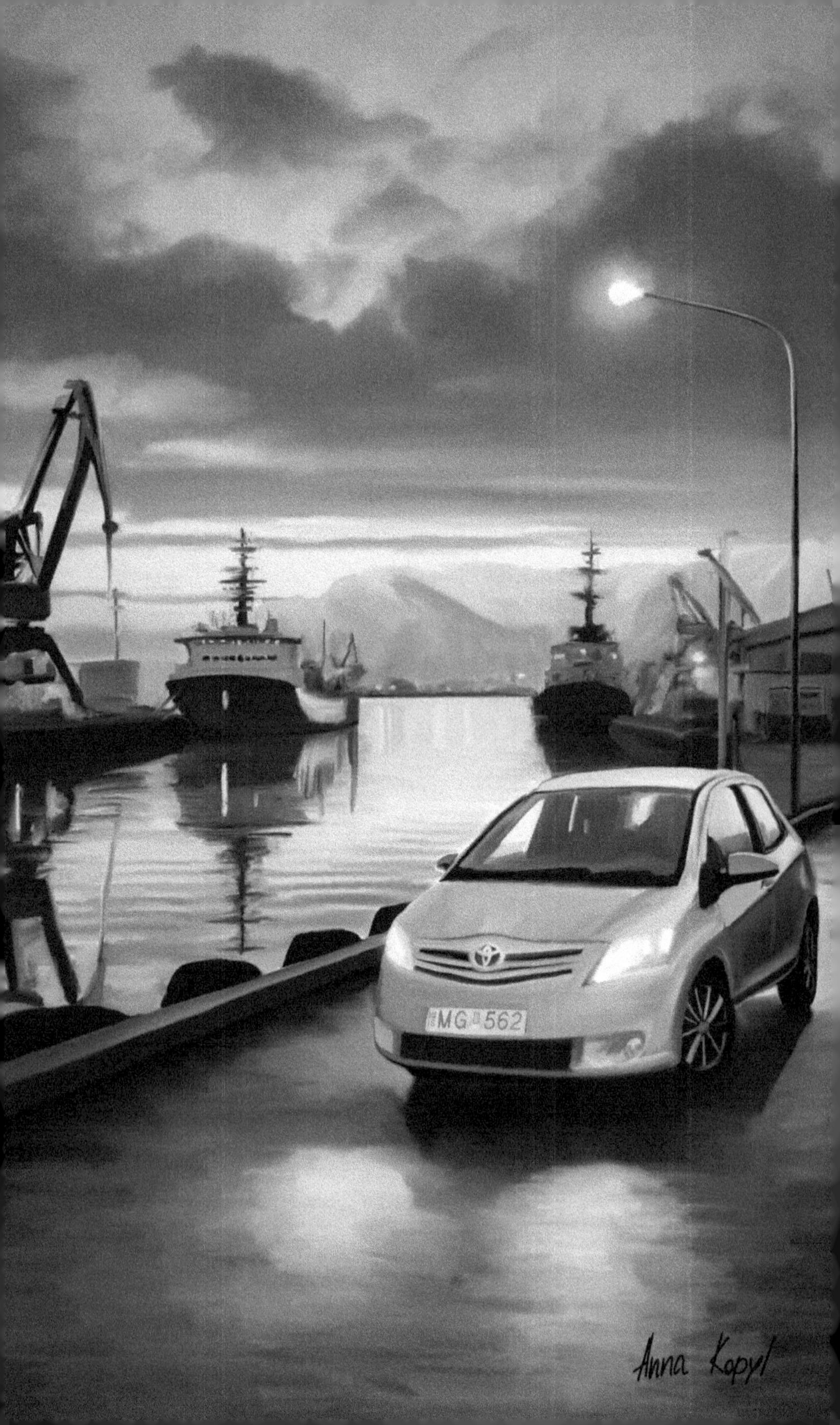
MG 562
Anna Kopyl

Summer in Reykjavík isn't as cold as most people think. The temperature ranges from 8°C to 16°C, and sometimes it can get up to 19°C. It rains almost every day, but the sun makes frequent appearances too, to the delight of locals and tourists. But despite the sometimes sun, a harsh, cold wind constantly comes in off the Atlantic. As the Icelandic saying goes: "If you don't like the weather, wait five minutes and it'll get even worse."

Danylo was on his way from the port of Reykjavík to the town of Garðabær,15 minutes away – essentially a Reykjavík suburb – in his old Toyota Auris. Danylo has been living and working in Iceland for the past ten months. It was the one-year anniversary of Kostia Khriashch's death, or rather his murder. Danylo stopped by a Wine Budin store on his way home, the only local chain where you could buy alcohol; regular grocery stores are stocked only with non-alcoholic beers. Danylo bought a bottle of Absolut vodka and a six-pack of Faxe beer. He would honor his friend's memory.

Danylo lived in an luxury private neighborhood, in a mansion that was being renovated by the firm that employed him. He worked as a translator from English, which most people in Iceland spoke as a second language. He was also in charge of purchasing and taking in the stock of building materials for the firm. It was a Ukrainian-Icelandic business: Ukrainian workforce and building materials, but Icelandic commissions and rates. How could it make sense to import building materials to Iceland from Eastern Europe? Prices for the same products in Iceland were at least four – and sometimes up to ten – times greater. Danylo's neighbors included a millionaire bank owner, Reykjavík's prosecutor general, a former education minister, and the owner of one of the largest fishing firms in Iceland – quite the mix.

When Danylo got back to his mansion that night, his colleague and roommate Borys Velychko was waiting for him on the balcony. He waved at Danylo and Danylo waved back. Borys was a foreman, a real construction professional. He was wise and had hands of gold. At 55, Borys was a family man with three kids – pretty old-school, a real good guy, Danylo thought. Oleh Velychko, Borys's nephew, also lived with them. He was Borys's assistant, his left hand, someone Borys could boss around and trust to get things done. Because Oleh was family, Borys felt obliged to look after him and help him where he could. Oleh's dad, Borys's brother, was a drunk; Oleh's mom divorced his dad, remarried, started a new family, and all but turned a blind eye to the son from her first marriage. Borys took his nephew under his wing when he saw that Oleh was running the risk of falling into addiction and ruining his life. Oleh was still young, not yet twenty. Danylo went inside and found Oleh in the kitchen, cooking pasta and lamb chops for everyone for dinner.

"I'm pouring us all shots," Danylo said. "Today's the anniversary of a close friend's death."

"Of course, Danylo," Borys replied. "Wash your hands and sit down, the kid's almost done making dinner." He had a way of sounding both fatherly and respectful.

"I'll only have one," Oleh said, "and no more. I've got lots of work tomorrow, I have to finish the tiles in the upstairs bathroom." Oleh was always trying to please his uncle.

After dinner, Oleh went up to his room to watch Narcos, and Danylo and Borys stay in the kitchen, which was at that point nearly done. There was almost no furniture there yet, except a large granite island in the middle of the room where Danylo and Borys sat.

"Danylo, you never told me how you got all the way up north to Iceland. You're not like the other guys who come looking for work. I saw that as soon as I met you. Trust me – I got experience with this stuff. I was even in jail for a couple years when I was younger. Took me a while to get my act together," Borys said. "Everyone who comes here for work is desperate to get back home three months later, and you've been here over six months and don't seem particularly hot on going back to Ukraine..."

"It's a long story," Danylo answered. "I'll tell you one day, but not today."

"Whatever you say. But tell me what your friend's name was, the one who died. I'll pour us another shot each but then I'm out. I can feel myself getting drunk."

"His name was Kostia. He was a good guy, did what was right, and always stood by his friends. There aren't many people like him. Let's honor his memory!"

The clinking of their shot glasses rang through the bare kitchen.

"Don't stay up too late Danylo, we've got four sites to visit tomorrow," Borys said.

"I'll do my best."

After Borys retired, Danylo drank another shot of vodka and went out into the courtyard. He pulled his phone out of his pocket and dialed Sasha Tarnavskyi.

"Hey, how are you?" Danylo asked when Sasha picked up. "How's Rome, the eternal city? We haven't talked in ages! Do you remember what day it is today?"

"Hi dude," Sasha said. "Well, things are alright. I miss home and I miss my family. I changed jobs; we're now doing security for a club in the very center of Rome, so I'm making a bit more money – at least there's that. And of course I remember. May Kostia rest in peace. I think about him a lot. Have you heard any news from Ukraine? I hope it's all quiet and no one's looking for us."

"Thankfully everything seems to be okay for now. Quiet. And I hope that's how things will stay. I heard that the case on Kostia's murder hasn't been closed yet, but I don't think they'll ever find his murderer, let alone the people behind the murder. Hennadii Trofimov and his KGB cronies have powerful people protecting them. He won't forget his son's death either, so we've got to stay careful. You still in touch with Bot and the others?"

"We texted recently," Sasha said, sighing. "Bot is in the mountains in the west of Ukraine, working as a developer. All he needs is a laptop and Internet connection, and he can work from anywhere in the world. Serhii and Hrisha are both in Prague, and Vova and Andrii are in Ivano-Frankivsk. Do you know anything about Doronin? And you still haven't said how you're doing."

"I heard that Doronin's Swedish boyfriend can't accept that Doronin hanged himself. He hired a private detective. Let's see what they manage to find. Kostia's people are monitoring the situation, I'll let you know if anything happens. Otherwise yeah, I'm great," Danylo said. "Iceland's a quiet place. I drive around Reykjavík in the evenings, the nature's really scenic here. I'll send you some photos! I'm so grateful to Diana for introducing me to Magnus and helping me find this job."

"By the way, my wife just told me that Diana gave birth recently. Had you heard?"

"No, she hasn't even posted any pictures from her pregnancy on social media. We were messaging on Instagram a couple of weeks ago, but she didn't mention it. Not even a hint! Very odd. Anyway, I think I'm going to head to bed. Was good to hear from you! Call soon."

"Same here, stay in touch!" Sasha said, hanging up.

Danylo and Borys set out on work errands at seven the next morning. First, they stopped in Hafnarfjörður, then Kópavogur, then Reykjavík, and then they went back to Garðabær, each town at most twenty kilometers from the next. An old building near the church in the very center of Hafnarfjörður, a charming port town, had recently been converted into a hostel. Danylo's firm was importing Ukrainian furniture to outfit the hostel. Now, a couple of men employed by the firm were putting all this furniture together: two kitchens, several wardrobes and cupboards, tables and chairs, nightstands, sofas, and a shitload of bunk beds. The men worked day and night, and it increasingly looked like they'd meet the deadline. Borys, usually strict and demanding, was pleased. Kópavogur –the second largest city in Iceland after Reykjavík, and practically a metropolis by Icelandic standards – had its own skyscraper and the largest shopping mall in Iceland to boot. Danylo's firm was just starting renovations on the façade of a four-story building there, but the brigade in charge of the works, headed by Stepan Miroshnyk, was a source of constant trouble. Stepan desperately wanted Borys's job and was prepared to do anything to set him up and push him out. Borys knew about Stepan's spiteful and devious intentions and was usually able to stave off Stepan's plots and put him in his place. Stepan was like a hyena; he acted stealthily and avoided open confrontation but could never accept being number two. His brigade always did their work well, but they often had trouble meeting deadlines. Because they were always running late, Borys or Danylo had to visit the sites where they worked every morning and evening to make sure they weren't slacking. Borys and Danylo's third stop, Reykjavík, the capital of Iceland, was a city of proud, but always friendly, Vikings. A harsh northern city that seemed filled with good magic. Not far from Harpa, the legendary and truly amazing concert hall, there was a fish restaurant called Whale's Appetite: two men from Ukraine's Zhytomyr region were resurfacing the restaurant's spacious and cozy terrace. Danylo and Borys made sure that everything there was going well and then went back to Garðabær for their most important job: Eiður Sigthórsson's mansion. As Deputy Director of the Keflavík International Airport, Iceland's largest, Sigthórsson was a big deal. His wife, Hrafnhildur, worked in fashion and was one of Iceland's most famous and popular designers. Both were public figures, and Magnus Gunnarsson, Danylo's employer, was very concerned with the quality of the work and reputation of his firm. He understood that everyone in Iceland knew each other, and his famous clients could make or break his business depending on whether they were pleased with the results of his work. Like most creatives, Hrafnhildur was whimsical and capricious, and her husband went to great lengths to please her. It took her more than two weeks to settle tiles for the kitchen; she changed her mind a truly incomprehensible number of times. Shop assistants would break into a cold sweat when they saw her. Six different types of tiles were delivered to the house at different points and subsequently returned. Four times she seemed to have made up her mind, and the brigade laid the tiles, only to have to undo their work the next day. Mrs Hrafnhildur would make unannounced visits to the site, call her husband and argue with him in Icelandic – then switch to English and politely tell Borys's workers that the tiles were not at all to her liking and had to be replaced. That was how the work on the Sigthórsson mansion proceeded. At least the pay was good, and the drama could actually be pretty entertaining.

Magnus Gunnarsson has worked in construction for a long time. At first, he'd worked with partners in Poland, but eventually decided that the ratio of pay to quality of work didn't quite make sense to him, so he started working with Ukrainians instead. He visited Kyiv, struck a deal with Ukraine's largest construction hypermarket, and found several partners who were now helping him find workers across Ukraine. Gunnarsson was in his early forties and had two divorces behind him. He flirted relentlessly and, despite his beer belly, was popular with the ladies.

Coincidentally, while Gunnarsson was in Kyiv, Danylo had been on his Desperados mission in Russian-occupied territory in the Donetsk region. As Danylo and his team were closing in on Panchyshyn's drug lab in Yasynuvata, Roman, the sympathetic Ukrainian Armed Forces officer, had received a phone call from Kostia Khriashch. On that call, Kostia had sounded particularly assertive and brusque.

Roman looked at Danylo, "Kostia says your operation is over – go back to your base."

A couple hours after the call, Danylo and his crew turned back toward Kyiv. They received no explanation of what had caused the hasty decision. The only thing they knew is that they had to be back in Kotsiubynske as soon as possible. The rest of the Desperados – Sasha Tarnavskyi and his team – were all there. Kostia convened a meeting. He paid them and told them to disappear and forget about everything that had happened. After the meeting, Sasha told Danylo that his ex Diana was in Kyiv, and Danylo decided to ask her if he could hole up in her flat for a while. She said yes. That was where Danylo met Alyona, Diana's friend who worked for Magnus Gunnarsson as a recruiter. Long story short, Danylo ended up on the other side of the world, in the land of volcanoes and ice.

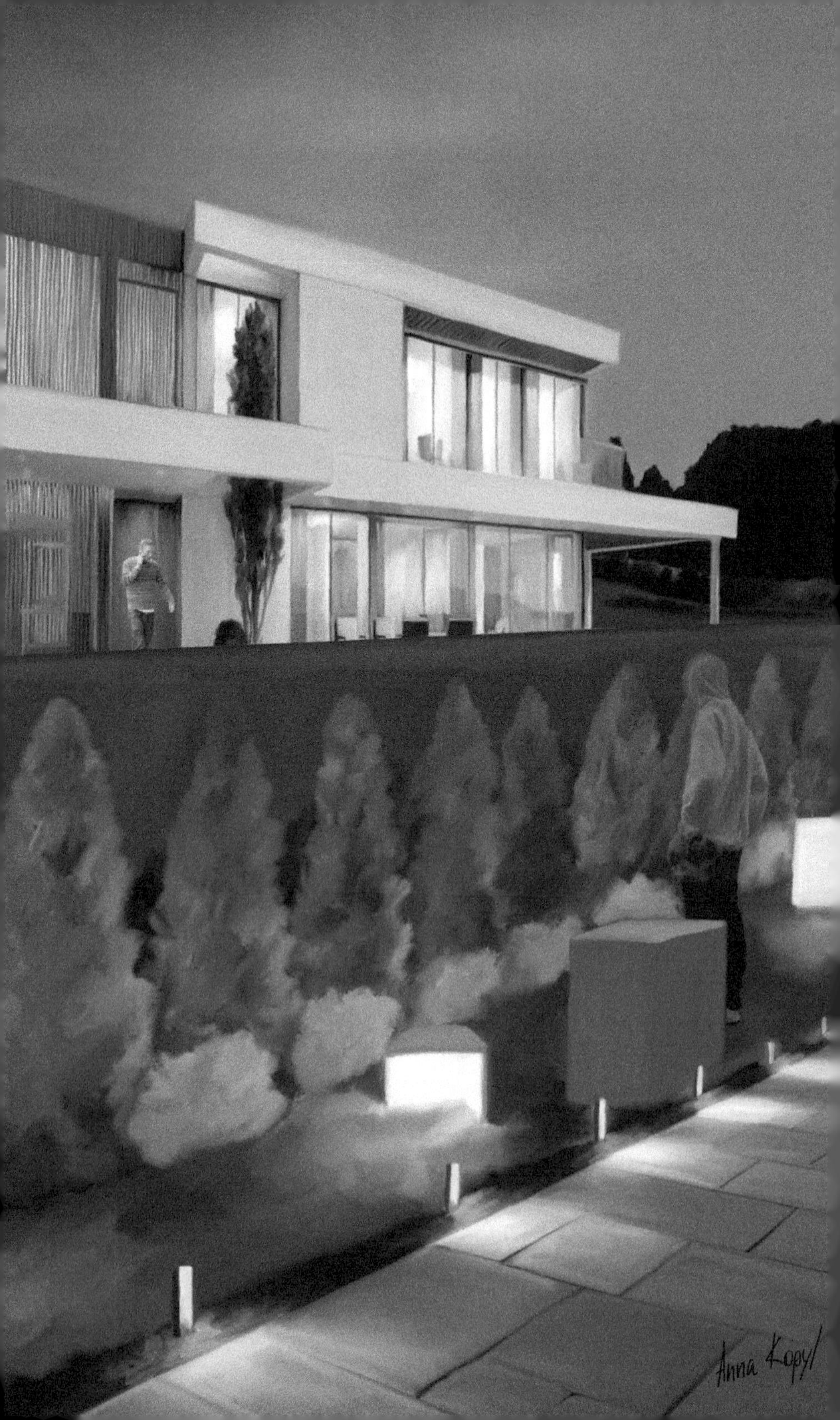
Anna Kopyl

Danylo stepped outside for a cigarette before going to bed on a light-filled summer evening – from May to August, the light never quite fizzles out of an Iceland night. He overheard someone speaking English in the neighbor's courtyard. That piqued his interest, and he listened in, almost involuntarily. He realized that the person whose voice he heard was Hjörtur Skúlason, owner of the fishing company. Skúlason sounded like he was desperately making excuses to whoever was on the other end of the line. He kept repeating that he would set everything right and would meet his interlocutor face-to-face in a week. Danylo knew something was off.

After the kitchen was finally tiled at the Sigthórsson mansion, Hrafnhildur held a small party for the workers. She prepared traditional Icelandic dishes for them. There was mutton soup; *hákarl*, dried and fermented shark; and *hvalspik*, or whale blubber, something of an equivalent to Ukrainian cured *salo*. There was booze, too. As the night progressed, Hrafnhildur started talking about their Garðabær neighbors. When it came to Skúlason and his fishing empire, she said he was involved in murky affairs and was able to make a fortune because of his criminal connections and not because of his business acumen. She shared with them a rumor that in addition to fresh fish, Skúlason traded in drugs and contraband. This stuck in Danylo's mind, and he thought back on Skúlason's phone call that night and began to keep an ear out for the businessman. He came up with an audacious plan.

***

Every day after work, Danylo went to a gym in Kópavogur. He did cardio, then swam in an open-air pool, which had a scenic view, and then spent fifteen minutes in the Finnish sauna. It was a way to pass time for him. Most people in Iceland lead rather boring lives and stayed in on cold, rainy evenings, reading or watching TV. Exercising was a popular way to mix things up. There was a girl at the gym Danylo went to that he liked. Her name was Alda. Her name was Icelandic for wave, and she was slender, fit, and very pretty. To himself he called her Bambi, because of her large green eyes that made him forget about everything else. Danylo had been around her for two long months but couldn't find an excuse or the right moment to talk to her. One day, though, he got lucky. He headed to get groceries after the gym and saw Alda in the supermarket parking lot. As she tried to open the door of her blue Mini Cooper, her grocery bag slipped out of her hands, spilling across the concrete. Danylo knew it was time to make a move.

"A beautiful girl like you shouldn't be carrying heavy bags," he said, in English. "Allow me to help you."

"Yes, thanks – if you don't mind. I'd appreciate some help," Alda said, picking things up.

"What's your name?" Danylo asked. "Or is it a secret?" He wasn't going to miss a chance to flirt with her.

"No, not at all. And definitely not for my savior. My name's Alda. What's yours? You must not be from here." She replied playfully.

"I'm Danylo. And you're right, I'm from Ukraine, but I've lived here for a few months now. We actually go to the same gym, in Kópavogur."

"Oh, you must have great memory for faces, I don't remember seeing you there!" Alda was, in fact, lying.

"You have that bright orange swimsuit, don't you?" Danylo asked.

"It's peach-colored, actually," she said, smiling. "Thanks for your help. Have a nice evening."

"You too. See you!"

The encounter made Danylo happy as a clam. He couldn't stop thinking about Alda. The next time he saw her at the gym, he was more decisive and invited her for a coffee. She said she'd think about it and gave him her phone number. Danylo was in equal measure patient and persistent; he gave her two days to think about his offer, then called her and convinced her to meet with him; his stubborn Ukrainian temperament won her over. His life took on new, brighter, colors. His attitude to both his work and the people around him changed dramatically. He was always smiling and content. Alda had given him a new lease on life. They travelled around Iceland together on the weekends.

They thought that the beauty of the country couldn't be contained in words; it was like another planet, another world. Danylo and Alda travelled across the

Golden Circle and visited every sightseeing spot: the Althing (Alþingi) parliament, one of the oldest in the world; Gullfoss Falls and the Öxarárfoss waterfall; Geysir and Strokkur geisers; the Kerið volcano crater lake; and countless other places. Alda Finnbogadóttir was studying psychology at Reykjavík University, the oldest and largest university in Iceland. In the summer she worked as a waitress in town. Her parents owned a souvenir shop in the city center and were quite well-off. Alda, however, refused to work in the family business, in large part because of her strained relationship with her parents. Her dad was a difficult person, and besides, he was conservative and old-fashioned. He couldn't even accept his daughter's chosen profession. Alda's mother was more lenient in private, but in public she always took her husband's side.

On the outside, it seemed that Danylo's life had turned around. He had a good job that paid well and had met a girl he liked. But somewhere inside, Danylo couldn't settle. He was thirsty for the thrill of dangerous plots. Maybe he was addicted to the risk. So Danylo started spying on the fishing magnate Hjörtur Skúlason's house. He noticed that a dark-green Land Rover Defender would show up there every couple of days. Two burly young men would get out of the car, both with distinct British accents, and go into the house, where they would stay for no longer than fifteen minutes. Once, an older man, probably in his seventies, came with the other two. He was tall and thin, and seemed to be the center of their attention. This man, with his gray hair and neat look, immediately caught Danylo's eye; he had a particular gravitas about him.

Danylo couldn't shake the urge to get inside Skúlason's house and figure out what was going on there. He was certain that what he would find there would be much more interesting than money. But how could he get in without incriminating himself? He had to get Borys's help. Borys had been a thief when he was younger and knew a thing or two about breaking into people's homes. Danylo had to find the right words to convince Borys. He invited him to have dinner and craft beer at the Pot-Bellied Konung in Reykjavík, where Alda worked as a waitress. The restaurant was pricey and in the city center. It served authentic Icelandic dishes and was popular with tourists, small but with an intimate, homely atmosphere. The waiters were always friendly and welcoming, there were barrels full of fresh beer brewed by local producers, and the signature lamb dish was famous across Iceland. The restaurant owner was partial to Alda because she was a diligent worker, always looked presentable, and her toothpaste-advert smile struck every visitor right in their heart, like a Cupid's arrow.

One night, Oleh drove Danylo and Borys to Pot-Bellied Konung. They arrived around eight, had dinner and a couple beers each, and then shots of potato brennivín. They talked about work over dinner and gossiped about their co-workers, but Borys knew they were there for a reason.

"Danylo, I'm obviously glad that you bought me this delicious dinner and introduced me to your girlfriend, but I know something's up, so why don't you just tell me what's going on," he said. "Are you getting married? Do you need money? You can just tell me now!"

"Well," Danylo said, "I am thinking about getting married in the future, but there's something else I wanted to talk to you about today. To be honest, I don't know where to start…"

"Just say it how it is."

"Okay, then hear me out – don't interrupt me – and then you can tell me what you think. Okay?"

"Fine, get on with it!" Borys said.

"I didn't come to Iceland on a whim." Danylo began, "I needed to get as far out of Ukraine as I could, as quickly as possible. I worked with a few guys for someone who was a big deal… But somewhere along the way, everything went awry. I'll tell you about it another time," he paused. "Here's what I wanted to talk to you about though. I've been watching Hjörtur Skúlason's house for a while now, he's our neighbor in Garðabær. The fishing magnate. I overheard a phone call of his recently, which made me think that the rumors about him must be true. He really is involved in some murky stuff. Two British guys show up at his house every week to pick up cash. But I don't think money is the only thing going here – I can feel that something more important is at stake. Can you help me get into his house? I want to have a look around – I know I'll be able to find something there. And I'm sure I'll be able to get us some of that black-market cash too, I swear there's a shitload of it, no one will even notice any of it missing. And if he eventually does, what will he do about it? He definitely can't go to the police, or else he'd have to tell them that the money he made dealing drugs and doing other shady stuff went missing. Come on, Borys, you have to say yes! If we work together as a team, it'll be perfect. No one will even know that anything happened."

"Look, Danylo, I hear you. But if I'm honest, I thought you had a little more sense in you! You have no idea what you've got yourself involved in," Borys said, "so either you leave Iceland, or I tell Magnus what's on your mind. You have a week," Borys got up, glaring at Danylo, and strode out of the restaurant.

Alda, seeing the confrontation, came up to Danylo as soon as Borys left.

"What happened? Is everything okay?" she asked.

"Yes, everything's great, Borys just doesn't feel well. Maybe it's his blood pressure," Danylo replied, playing it off. "Old age is no fun. How much longer are you working for? Will you be able to give me a lift to Garðabær after work?"

"Not long, we're closing in half an hour. Of course I can give you a lift, but I want a thousand kisses in return."

"Of course, my Nordic princess, maybe even two thousand…"

Over the next couple of days, Danylo acted like nothing happened. He went to work, joked with his co-workers, and was friendly with everyone. Borys, on the other hand, iced Danylo out completely, constantly sulked around and took his bad mood out on workers. His nephew Oleh got the worst of it. Danylo hoped he'd be able to talk to Borys one-on-one at the swimming pool and resolve things amicably, but Borys refused to go with him. In response to all this, Danylo started to prepare for the worst-case scenario, but he still managed to keep his composure and didn't let on his unease.

On Friday, after a long week at work, Danylo decided to blow off steam and go for a run at a track at a local school. A man came to the track while he was running and sat down in the bleachers. Danylo could see at a distance that it was Borys. He finished his lap and walked off the track up into the bleachers.

"Hello Borys, here for a run?"

"You know, Danylo, I do love a good run, but it's not on my schedule today."

"Sure is funny to find yourself at a track, then. Maybe it's my humble self you're here for."

"I see you're not short of self-confidence – I hear it's trendy these days. But don't overdo it."

"Thanks for advice, I'll keep that in mind," Danylo said. "With all due respect, let's just get down to business."

"Fine. Let's talk," Borys said, crossing his arms. "The day after we had dinner, I got a call from my wife, who told me that during her latest medical check-up she was diagnosed with cancer. At first I was shocked, but I pulled myself together. Under any other circumstances, I would never get involved in this shitty plan of yours, but life has forced me to look at it from a different angle. I'm willing to help you you're your Skúlason plan. Oleh will help us too, you can count on him. He's not particularly smart, but he's reliable, and we can trust him. And he'll do anything for his beloved aunt, she's dearer to him than his own mother. Right, enough with the chit-chat. Do you have a plan? When do you want to start?"

"Don't worry, I've got a plan," Danylo said. "I've been thinking about this whole thing for a couple of weeks now, and I'm always watching Skúlason's house. How about I give you two hours to talk to Oleh and explain the situation to him, and then let's sit down the three of us and I'll run you through my plan, step by step? And of course if you have any comments and ideas, let me know. You're more experienced with this stuff."

"Fine. Fine. You should know that I also used to work for a firm that installed alarm systems and surveillance cameras. No one in Iceland has alarms because break-ins and theft are very rare – Magnus mentioned this to me the other day. But I saw that Skúlason has two cameras outside. I can handle that no problem."

***

Danylo, Borys, and Oleh met in the empty kitchen of their Garðabær home around eleven that night. Though it was late, the light was just fading into darkness. Danylo told the other two that Hjörtur Skúlason and his family pack their things into their luxury camper van, hitch it to their brand-new Volvo SUV, and head to a camping park every Friday afternoon; they don't arrive back until Sunday evening. Before Danylo laid out the plan, he suggested next Friday for carrying it out. By way of an alibi, he thought they should organize a staff party in Kópavogur, get everyone really drunk, and – while avoiding drinking themselves – pretend that they were also drunk. Garðabær was only a ten-minute drive from Kópavogur. Once back at the Garðabær house, Danylo and Borys would strike up some Ukrainian songs – the louder the better – to make their neighbors think they were drunk. Danylo hoped this would convince any looking into the matter that the simple migrant workers from Ukraine wouldn't physically have had the wherewithal to break into Skúlason's house unnoticed, even if they'd had some motive. Deep at night, when the residents of the luxury settlement would be dreaming about their ancestors returning to their native lands on formidably sized *drakkars*, or viking ships, Danylo and Borys, wearing masks, would enter Skúlason's house through the backyard.

***

The week went by in a flash – suddenly it was Friday. Borys convinced their boss Magnus to throw a staff party, and Hjörtur Skúlason and his family were off to admire Iceland's nature and spend time with friends. So far, all was going according to Danylo's plan. At around 2:30am, Oleh took up his post by a window on the second floor of the house in Garðabær. His task was to keep watch. If he spotted something suspicious, he was to call Danylo and say: "I'm feeling awful, call an ambulance." Meanwhile, Danylo and Borys quietly approached the fence that circled Skúlason's backyard. Borys used a table and a stool to climb over the fence and cut a corrugated gray pipe that housed the power cable for the CCTV cameras. Borys gave Danylo the all-clear, and Danylo quickly scaled the fence into Skúlason's backyard. They wasted no time, using a crowbar to smash the garage window and enter the house, where they parted ways. Danylo rifled through cupboards and drawers, looking for information and leads that could be useful in the future, while Borys, a real jack-of-all-trades, looked for money like a hound sniffing out prey. Above the fireplace, among other pictures on a living room wall, Danylo saw a picture of Skúlason with the tall gray-haired man he'd seen at the house a couple of weeks ago. Underneath the photo a caption read: "An unforgettable fishing trip to Flatey Island." Danylo's eyes raked through the rest of the pictures before moving on to Skúlason's office. On his desk was an enormous iMac Pro with a yellow post-it note in the middle of the screen. On it was scrawled: "Flatey – Úlfur, URGENT." Borys's voice broke the strangely mystical silence of the room, and Danylo shuddered.

"Hey Danylo, come on over," Borys called out. "I'm in the fisherman and his mermaid's bedroom!"

"Coming, just a second," Danylo said, already on his way. "What'd you find?"

"A safe that there's no fucking way we can open. But I also went through their dirty laundry…"

"And what'd you find there?" Danylo asked, hushed. "Come on, tell me, stop dragging your feet!"

"I found a trash bag stuffed with dollar bills at the bottom of the drawer. The thug's safe must be so chock-full that there was no room left for the cash!"

"Holy fuck, amazing! Let's cover our tracks and get the fuck out of here."

"Yes sir, let's get out quick," Borys said, nodding quickly.

There was 70,000 dollars in the bag – less than what they hoped for, but better than nothing. Danylo and Borys took 33,000 each and gave the remaining 4,000 to Oleh, to keep his mouth shut.

As Danylo had predicted, Skúlason didn't make a fuss about the disappearance of the cash. The magnate didn't want the police to take an interest in his affairs. The head of Reykjavík's police department had recently been replaced, and Skúlason knew it would cost him less to stay silent about the theft, lay low, and grow more careful and watchful than ever. Meanwhile, Danylo, Borys, and Oleh acted as though nothing had happened; they never talked about their rummage through Skúlason's house.

Danylo had been planning a trip to Húsavík on the northeast coast of Iceland for a couple of weeks. He wanted to go on a famous whale-watching boat tour and take pictures. But after the heist, he couldn't get the mysterious Flatey Island out of his head. It beckoned to him like siren song. Danylo scoured Google and YouTube for information. Flatey Island was a tiny island in the Atlantic Ocean, forty kilometers off the coast of Iceland. It could be reached by ferry from Stykkishólmur three times a week. Only a few dozen people lived on the island. On it was the oldest – and smallest – library in Iceland, home to only a hundred books. Tourists gravitated to the island May through August because of the annual migration of puffins, handsome black-and-white birds with large bright-colored beaks. Danylo became obsessed with visiting Flatey Island, and it didn't take much effort for him to convince Alda to go there instead of their planned trip to Húsavík: puffins, after all, won over whales. But it wasn't the island's natural beauty or historic significance that Danylo was interested in.

Before their trip, Danylo went to the 66north store to buy a few things for himself and his girlfriend. It was a popular brand with tourists traveling through Iceland, and he thought the gear would help them keep a low profile on Flatey Island. He bought two stylish and comfortable jackets: an orange one for himself and one in light green for Alda. He also bought a baseball cap and a warm woollen hat. By European standards, 66north stuff was far from cheap. The jackets each set him back 500 dollars, but they were good-quality, stylish, and, crucially, warm for Iceland's rainy and cold weather. There was another reason Danylo had his eyes on those jackets: many tourists bought 66north clothes in Iceland, and he hoped that the gear he bought would help him blend in with the crowds and not attract too much attention.

Danylo and Alda left for the island on a Friday afternoon. She had a day off and Danylo asked Borys to leave work a couple hours early. Alda picked Danylo up from Garðabær. As he loaded his bags into the trunk of Alda's car for their three-day trip, Eva, his neighbor from across the street, the sixteen-year-old girl daughter of Reykjavík's prosecutor general, approached him.

"Hey, looks like you're leaving for the weekend," she said to Danylo.

"Hi. Yes, we're going on a little trip to see some parts of the country we haven't seen before."

"My brother Guðmundur said he saw someone break into Hjörtur Skúlason's house," she said. "But don't worry, even if it was one of you guys, we won't tell anyone. My family can't stand the Skúlasons." With that, Eva smiled, turned, and walked away.

Danylo looked as though a bucket of cold water had been dumped on him while he was standing naked in the cold. Shocked, he got into the car. Alda asked him what Eva had wanted.

"She wanted to know where we were going for the weekend," Danylo said.

"What's wrong with your face?" Alda asked. "You seem worried. You were smiling and joking a second ago, and now you've got the long face of a student who's about to take an exam he hasn't studied for." She knew Danylo well, and her psychology classes always helped her read him.

"No no, honey, everything's alright."

"Isn't she the daughter of Reykjavík's prosecutor general? I think you told me about her. You guys call her Little Gangsta, don't you? She's the one who blasts hip-hop whenever her parents leave the house?"

"That' right, that's her! Her mom is always mad at her because she loves to throw a party for her friends, and the neighbors always complain about the noise."

"Doesn't she have an older brother? Isn't he on the autism spectrum?"

"Yes, I think he's just over twenty. He hardly leaves the house, poor guy," Danylo mumbled, pulling off the road. "Let's get some gas and a coffee."

"Yes, let's! I'm feeling tired, wouldn't mind a boost of energy," Alda said, stretching in her seat.

On almost two hundred kilometers to Stykkishólmur Danylo tried to act normal. It was a skill of his, but still Alda knew something was wrong, and though she didn't bring it up again, she was hatching a plan of her own. Halfway to their destination, Danylo told her that he'd like to nod off for half an hour. He closed his eyes but couldn't stop replaying Eva's words in his head. Eva's brother Guðmundur really was on the spectrum; everyone in Garðabær knew that he was often out at night and it wasn't a surprise to run into him. Eva and Guðmundur had a strained relationship with the Skúlason family because Hjörtur Skúlason often played cruel jokes on Guðmundur. In retaliation, Guðmundur sometimes inflicted minor damage on Skúlason's property. Danylo knew all of this, but it hadn't occurred to him that Eva's brother could have been there on the night he and Borys broke into the house, unnoticed as he crouched between a trampoline and an enormous gas grill on the other side of the Skúlason's yard.

By the time Danylo and Alda got to Stykkishólmur, they felt too tired to explore the quaint fishing town. They headed straight to their hotel, where they had dinner and a couple beers, and went to bed. They parked their car at a lot early the next morning and headed to the 7:00am ferry. An hour and a half later, they were on Flatey Island. They dropped their things off at the Westfjords hotel, the only one on the island, and went out to explore the small island. There was a special atmosphere on Flatey, incredibly calm, thanks to the Atlantic Ocean and the fjords. Ostensibly their main reason for visiting the island was to find the famous puffin colonies and take as many pictures of them as possible. But Danylo also had another goal, and his intuition told him that he was on the right track. He disguised himself well: he wore his hood, a hat, and a pair of sunglasses.

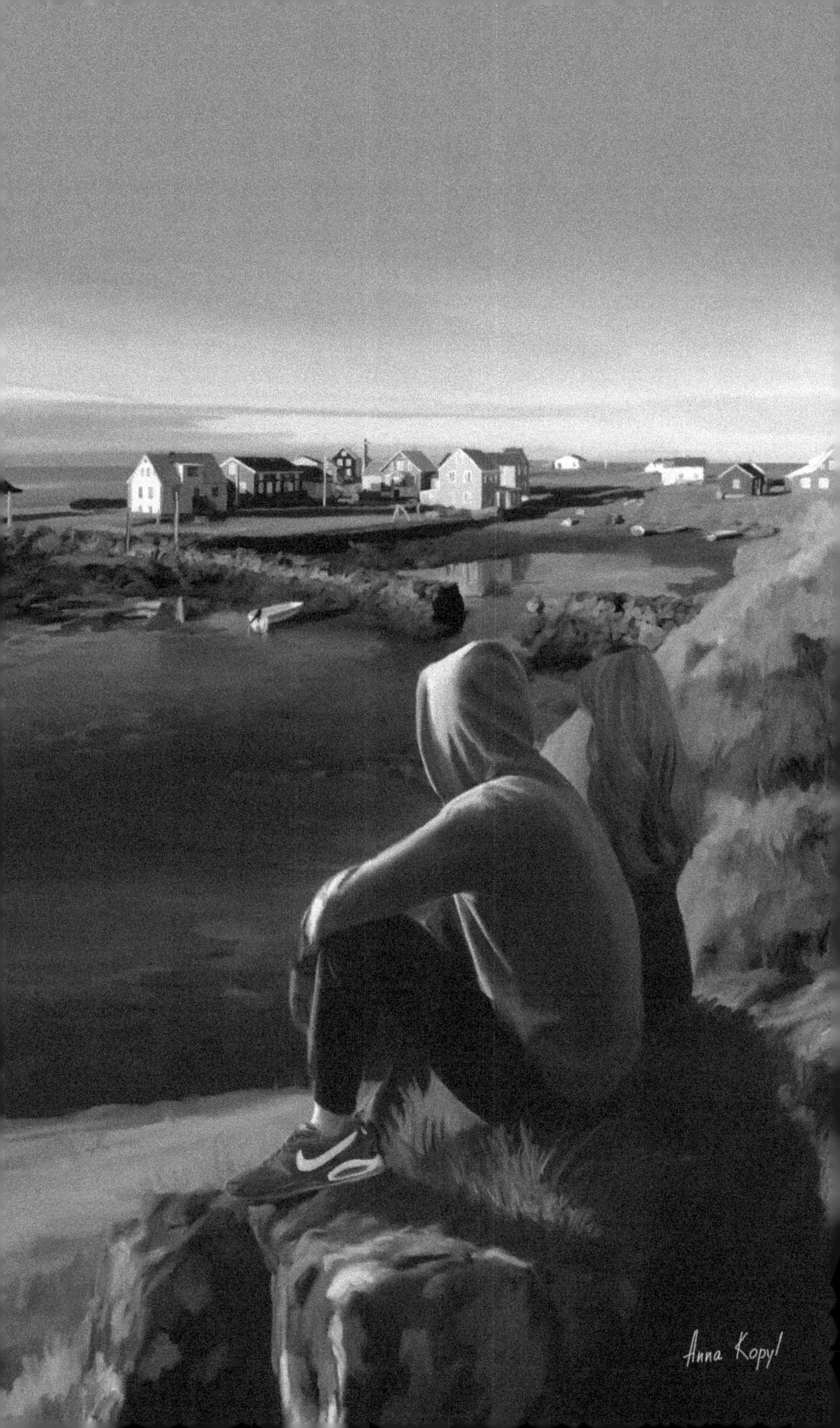
Anna Kopyl

The wind blew strong on the island, with the sun occasionally sliding through the clouds, so his look wasn't out of place. After spending two hours taking pictures of puffins, and Alda, against the scenic backdrop of the island, Danylo suggested they head back to the village and take pictures of the local lifestyle. She agreed happily. They first visited an old and very quiet church and then went for a walk among the few brightly painted houses. A sheep farm sat next to one house, and Danylo told Alda they should get closer and take some pictures of the sheep. This house stood apart from others. It was bigger and had a large porch. Next to it was a small guest house and several storage buildings – it was properly a ranch. Two young men sat on the porch. As Danylo got close enough to see their faces, he realized that they were the same men he saw accompanying the tall, older man on his visit to Skúlason a few weeks back. Danylo's looked on through the lens of his camera, intrigued. He managed to hide his agitation from Alda, and after she took at least a hundred pictures of sheep, they went back to their hotel, where they had delicious and freshly caught Atlantic seafood for lunch. They went on a short walk along the island's tiny beach before deciding to retire to their room to rest for a couple hours before heading to a bar that evening. By seven that night, they were sitting at the bar in the island's only drinking establishment. Both were happy.

"My beloved Alda, what would you like to drink on this wonderful evening?"

"I don't know, sweetheart. I think I'd like something strong, but maybe I'll start with a mojito, and then we'll see… I'm planning on tapping into my wild Viking roots later. Maybe I'll be laying siege to your fortress all night," Alda said, then kissed Danylo on the lips, passionately but tenderly.

"Well, if you're going to act like Lagertha tonight, I better get myself ready. I'll have a whisky."

While the two discussed their plans for the night, the bartender quietly approached them, without their noticing. He was tall and bold and had a pale blond stubble. His face was rough, but he had kind eyes. He wore a red-and-black plaid shirt with the sleeves rolled up to his elbows, and his arms were covered in tattoos.

"Good evening. Are you ready to order? What would you like?" the bartender asked.

"Hello, my friend," Danylo said. "We'll start with a double rum mojito and a double shot of whisky – your choice – on the rocks. Choose well!"

"My job is to please."

Danylo drained his glass in half an hour. Alda took longer: she was busy talking, gossiping about her friends and about her dad's difficult temperament. Danylo summoned the bartender again when they had both finished:

"Excuse me, could I order more drinks?"

"Just a moment, coming!" the bartender called.

"I'll have the same, but with more ice and soda," Alda told Danylo.

The bartender returned to them a couple minutes later.

"What would you like? I hope you enjoyed the whisky?"

"Yes, great choice, thank you," Danylo said. "Can we have the same again, just more ice and soda in the mojito please? And get yourself a drink too and join us when you can. We don't get to visit beautiful islands like this everyday, we'd be curious to talk to someone who lives here."

"Thank you, I'm glad you liked it. Let me just serve those Americans over there, and then I'll gladly join you."

"Great, we're in no rush."

As soon as the bartender walked away again, Alda said, annoyed, "I don't understand why you want to talk to him. Can't you just Google it if you want to know something about the island? You can find anything on there. To be honest, I don't want to share you with anyone else."

"My darling Alda, don't get mad. I won't keep him long, maybe fifteen minutes? I'm curious to talk to him. Bartenders usually know more than a search engine, all the mysteries and rumors and legends. Flatey seems to me like a very mysterious place."

"Fine, but not longer," Alda said, drawing the line. "Otherwise I'll just get up, go to our room, and lock the door, and you can spend the night with your new amigo. And you know what, Danylo? It's not the island that's mysterious, but you, for the second day now."

"Okay my queen – deal. I'm just lost in how wonderful our trip has been so far," Danylo smiled, trying to please Alda with flattery.

The bartender came back over and spoke to them with genuine enthusiasm.

"Welcome to Flatey Island, friends. My name's Erik. And yours? Where are you from?"

"Hello Erik. My name's Daniel, and this is Ingrid. We're from Canada. We've always wanted to visit Iceland, and finally our dream has come true."

"Congratulations! What are your plans? Do you need any recommendations?" Erik asked.

"We've travelled around the Golden Circle and are spending two days here on Flatey now. We'd like to visit Húsavík next. You've got so much going on here, on your tiny island: a hotel, a restaurant, a port, a beach, two farms, a church, a library. Everything's so close together. What a wonderful place. Do you live here year-round?"

"No, I'm here late April through about the middle of September, then I go back to Stykkishólmur. My family owns this bar and hotel, and I'm just helping with the family business. What are your thoughts on Iceland so far?"

"It's better than I imagined," Danylo replied. "And by the way, I wanted to ask. There's a large red house not far from here, next to a sheep farm. I was wondering if the owner rents rooms out to visitors?"

"Oh no, he doesn't. The house is owned by the local tycoon, Úlfur Rúnarsson, a former military man. He also owns a barn and a fishing boat, the largest one around here. He served in the NATO forces and moved here after retiring from the military. He's a local hero."

"Wow, crazy, what an interesting cast of characters you've got here. Are there a lot of tourists here in the summer?" Danylo asked.

"Yes, quite a lot," Erik said, "they keep us busy. Most hotel rooms are booked all through the summer. People come from every corner of the world. No time to be idle. Would you like another drink?"

"No thank you, just the bill please. I think we're ready to retire for the night."

"Yeah, no problem. Thanks for coming! Have a nice evening."

"Thanks a lot, see you."

As soon as the bartender left them alone, Alda kicked Danylo in his leg.

"Hey, Agent 007, what was this? Canada? Ingrid?" she demanded.

"I just wanted to feel mysterious, do some acting… I thought you might enjoy it," Danylo whispered softly in her ear. Of course it hadn't just been for fun but was part of a plan he was hatching.

"I've never seen that side of you before," Alda said. "I have to say, you were quite convincing."

"Thank you. Now let's go upstairs. You've been a naughty girl, it's time for you to get a good spanking."

In front of the door to their room, Danylo turned Alda to face him and kissed her neck and lips. They were so turned on they barely managed to get into the room. When they did, Danylo pulled Alda's sweatshirt off, unhooked her bra, and started licking, biting, and caressing her breasts. Alda loved it; she moaned softly with pleasure. Once in bed, Danylo got Alda to kneel on all fours and entered her from behind. Her moans became louder and more animal.

The next morning, Danylo and Alda woke up to the howling of the wind outside their window. Storms over the Atlantic. They didn't want to get out of bed, but they had to make it to the buffet breakfast. After they ate, they headed for the ferry back to Stykkishólmur. Alda dropped Danylo off at Garðabær before driving on to Reykjavík. On Sundays, she always had dinner with her family, though she never looked forward to it. When Danylo got back to his room, he sat on the bed with his head in his hands. Anxious thoughts swarmed his mind, most urgent among them was what to do about the prosecutor's daughter Eva and her brother. It was a difficult question that required the most delicate and precise approach. Danylo figured it was better not to tell Borys and his nephew that Guðmundur saw them break into Skúlason's house. Borys might grow paranoid and deranged, do something stupid. Asking Eva what exactly her brother saw would mean admitting she was right in suspecting Danylo and his co-workers. Threatening the children of Reykjavík's prosecutor general would likely get Danylo, Borys, and Oleh imprisoned and cause an international scandal. Danylo was also worried about how much Alda heard – or guessed – when Eva spoke to him about the break-in her brother had witnessed. Did Alda think Danylo and his co-workers were involved? After hours of anxious thinking, Danylo felt beat down by the doubt and self-torment. He decided to lay low and see what would happen. If any complications arose, he would act in accordance with the circumstances.

Alda didn't like spending time with her family but agreed to do it her mom's sake – for her mom's peace of mind and her own. Her mom had heart issues, and Alda was doing her best to protect her from unnecessary worry. Spending an hour at the family table listening to her dad droning on and on about his knowledge, competence, and foresight was the least she could do. After dinner, Alda went up to her room. She was curious about what she heard Danylo's neighbor, the prosecutor's daughter, say a couple of days before that. It didn't take her long to find Eva's Instagram account – Garðabær isn't exactly a megapolis – and after an hour of scrolling, Alda found what she was looking for. She saw in Eva's stories that she was at the El Patrón bar with her friends. The bar, one of the most popular ones in Reykjavík, was close to Alda's house. Driven by her curiosity, she left her bed, got ready to go out, and set out for El Patrón. She sat at a table right next to Eva and her friends, ordered a cocktail, and started watching what was going on at the next table over. Eva and her two friends were drinking tequila with three guys who seemed a lot older than the teenage girls. The guys appeared to be American tourists, and the girls, already quite drunk, were sitting on their knees, making out after every shot they took like there was no tomorrow. Alda was caught off guard but didn't lose her cool. She took pictures of the girls and a short video. She stayed at her table a while longer. When Eva got up to use the restroom, Alda followed her there.

"I see you're having fun," Alda said to her in an accusatory tone.

"Who are you?" Eva asked calmly, "and what do you want from me?"

"It really doesn't matter who I am right now. What matters is who you are, and who your mother is. I took a couple of pictures that I think you wouldn't want your family to see."

"Okay," Eva said, seeming to sober up at Alda's words, "so what do you want?"

"I want very little. If you answer my question, we can both forget about this encounter once and for all. Deal?"

"Deal. Ask away."

"Your brother saw someone breaking into the house of your neighbor, Hjörtur Skúlason. Does he know who it was?"

"My brother has autism and doesn't tell anything to anyone other than me. He says they were construction workers from the building next to Skúlason's house, but I'm not sure."

"Thanks. And let me give you a bit of advice: call a taxi and go home."

Alda, who was usually charming and quiet, felt furious and determined; she sensed that Danylo was involved in the break-in. She went home, but couldn't sleep all night, haunted by thoughts about why Danylo would've done something this irresponsible and risky. She wanted to call him or go talk to him in Garðabær and settle everything that same night but changed her mind and decided that such an issue would be best handled with a cool head. A break-in was inexcusable, she thought, at least in her world. In the morning, Alda texted Danylo, saying that she wanted to meet him at eight that night, on the waterfront near the Harpa concert hall.

Danylo had also hardly gotten any sleep, twisting and turning until the early morning, when he finally nodded off for a couple of hours. When his alarm woke him up at seven, he rolled out of bed with a terrible headache and very little will to live. He knew it would be a tough day. He kept returning, again and again, to the fact that he and Borys failed to notice Eva's brother in Skúlason's yard. How was that possible?

It was, indeed, a long day, and Danylo had a lot of work to get through. The workers at Kópavogur were running behind; one of the guys working on the terrace of the Whale's Appetite was sick with a fever, and the kitchen delivered to the Hafnarfjörður hostel turned out to have all the wrong measurements and dimensions. Danylo was absorbed into dealing with all this, and in the thick of work forgot about the prosecutor's daughter, her brother, the break-in, and even his worriers about Alda. He didn't have time to think about his meeting with her that night, to imagine where their conversation might go. Once done with work, he drove to Reykjavík, grabbed some food at the first fast food restaurant he saw, and rushed to meet Alda. A nasty wind, cold and piercing, was tearing through the city, chilling everyone to the bone. Only a few tourists loitered in front of the concert hall. Danylo wanted to give Alda a hug when he saw her, but she drew away from him(;) (.) (she wanted to show him there was no time for displays of affection.)

"Danylo, I've got to talk to you about something, and it's not going to be a very nice conversation. But you have to promise that you'll be completely honest with me."

"First of all, hi," Danylo said. "Let's talk. I'm always honest with you."

"Tell me the truth, were you involved in the break-in into Hjörtur Skúlason's house?"

"I don't know what you're talking about. What break-in? Who the hell is Hjörtur?"

"I knew it…" Alda muttered to herself.

"I don't understand what you're talking about! Please, just, explain."

"You want me to explain? Fine, I'll explain! Yesterday I talked to Eva, the prosecutor's daughter, and she told me her brother saw two people from the house where you live entering Skúlason's house. How can you explain that? Do you have anything to do with this?" Alda asked, driving her finger into his chest.

"This is complete nonsense – it's the first time I've heard about this! Eva's brother has autism, he can make all kind of stuff up. You trust their word more than mine?" Danylo yelled, sticking to his version of events. He knew that dragging Alda into the mess he had started was dangerous.

"You know what, sweetheart, I heard some of your conversation with Eva just before we left for Flatey Island. I've known you for a while now, and my psychology degree also stood me a good stead. On our way to the island, you didn't act like yourself: you seemed all scared and sluggish and were quiet the whole way. I think you're lying to me. I would've been able to understand and accept a lot of things, but not your lies. I'm not going to tolerate them I'm sorry, but we have to stop seeing each other," Alda turned around and left Danylo. Shocked, he stood in the middle of the street, silently staring after her. The cruel wind from the Atlantic lashed at his body and his face.

He went back to Garðabær. The situation was out of his control now, and he knew it. He had two choices: either leave everything be and pray that it would turn out okay or go all in and risk everything. Danylo chose the latter. He decided to think out of the box and act boldly and swiftly. He was convinced that Úlfur

Rúnarsson and his men on Flatey Island were guarding something truly precious. He knew that he wouldn't be able just to go there and find out what it was – let alone steal it – on his own. What he needed was a plan and a group of three or four trustworthy men to implement it. A plan was already shaping up in Danylo's mind. He texted his old friends Sasha Tarnavskyi, Slava aka "Bot", Andrii, Vova, Hrisha, and Serhii – everyone involved in the Desperados – saying that he was getting married and inviting them to his bachelor party in Iceland. He said he'd pay for their flights and accommodation. It was a tempting offer, he thought, betting also that the lie about getting married would make refusing it all the more uncomfortable. Andrii and Vova said they wouldn't be able to come because of work; Serhii said he wasn't sure and would reply later; Hrisha didn't respond at all. Sasha, however, said he would come and bring along an Italian friend. Bot also gladly agreed. Danylo set the date: August 24, Ukraine's Independence Day. He invited his friends to stay for three or four days. He knew it would take a while to get to Flatey Island, what with the long drive and the ferry crossing, and he still didn't know what exactly it was that Rúnarsson was hiding on the island. Money, precious stones, cocaine or other drugs, stolen art? It could've been anything.

Danylo dedicated himself to preparing before his friends' arrival. He withdrew money from his bank account, the $20,000 he kept in the Erion bank. He hid the rest of his savings in cash at the house in Garðabær. Then Danylo used his boss Magnus Gunnarsson's ID card to access Iceland's online ancestry tracing service, which went all the way back to Reykjavík's founder Ingólfur Arnarson. He came across a curious fact: Hjörtur Skúlason and Úlfur Rúnarsson were second cousins, and their family descended from British immigrants. Danylo rented accommodation and a new Volvo XC 60. All he had left to do was convince his friends to take part in his crazy plan.

The two weeks before their arrival flew by, and finally Bot, Sasha, and his friend Vincenzo arrived at the Reykjavík-Keflavík airport. Danylo hadn't heard from Alda since their argument. She didn't respond to his texts. It was as if they had never known one another. Danylo took a week off at work under the pretext that his family was visiting and he wanted to show them around Iceland. No one mentioned the break-in at Skúlason's house, and when his friends arrived, Danylo took them to the flat he had rented for them. Later that night, they headed to Austar, a popular Reykjavík club.

"Well, *ragazzi*," started Sasha, "here we are again together. Plenty of time has passed and a lot has changed since we last saw each other. I'm grateful to God that after everything we were involved in, we're all still here and alive. And I want to congratulate Danylo on his wedding, such an important event in anyone's life. I wish that you and your future wife will always love each other, that you're able to find compromises, and have lots of wonderful kids." Sasha was sincere and emotional while giving his toast.

"I wish you two to always be happy together," Vincenzo said in his Italian accent.

"My warmest wishes," Bot joined in, "I'm so happy for you." They all clinked their glasses together.

Danylo smiled and thanked his friends. They started on champagne, but soon switched to tequila. They met women from Poland, Spain, and Denmark, who were also in the club, and Danylo bought all of their drinks. Around two in the morning, Danylo's friends were ready to go back to their apartment with a group of Spanish women that Vincenzo had convinced to join them, but Danylo had other plans. They went back to the rented flat without the women and continued drinking there. Danylo decided it was time for him to get down to business.

"Guys, I hope you'll understand, but if you don't, that's okay too," he said. "I'm not actually getting married, and the bachelor party was just an excuse to get you all to Reykjavík. I know it's a dirty move, but I had no choice. Please hear me out. Then you can make up your own minds." Sasha and Bot went quiet. Vincenzo, who didn't speak Ukrainian, noticed the shift of atmosphere and looked at the others curiously. Danylo continued, "I heard rumors that my neighbor is not at all the businessman he pretends to be, but a hustler. I started watching his house and saw that every week he's visited by an older, respectable-looking guy and his two bodyguards. A friend and I broke into his house and found some cash there that we took, but I also found out that this other, older guy lives on Flatey Island, an island in the Atlantic some forty kilometers off the coast of Iceland. I went there to see it for myself, and learned that this guy served in the NATO forces and that – I'm telling you – he's hiding something very precious on this island. I want us to go there tomorrow and rob this guy."

"Fucking hell, you're a real fraud," Sasha said, the first to recover from the surprise. "We traveled across all of Europe to celebrate the fact that you finally got some sense in your head and were getting married and starting a family, such a serious step, a real man's step, and here you are! But you know what the strangest thing is?" he said, grabbing the bottle of champagne and gulping down what was left, "I'm in. Let's do it."

"What about your friend?" Danylo asked.

"Vincenzo Farinelli's family is from Sicily, so he won't need convincing…"

"I'm also here, by the way," Bot said. "You're always getting me into trouble. To hell with you! I'm coming too," he added and headed to his bedroom.

The next morning, a crowded ferry took the three Ukrainians and one Italian to Flatey Island, where they would try their luck. Sasha had a fake Romanian passport, which they used to rent a small cottage. The plan was to pretend that all four of them were Romanians who travelled to Iceland to learn about sheep farming and buy sheep that they would then breed in Romania. Icelandic sheep and their unique wool are famous the world over. It was a perfect excuse to meet Úlfur Rúnarsson. Danylo, Tarnavksyi, Bot, and Vincenzo went on a walk around the island, then got a bite to eat and headed straight to Rúnarsson's property. Once there, they feigned great interest in the sheep farm. Within ten minutes, a guard came out of the smaller house and rudely asked them what they were doing there. The four guys were prepared for this and politely asked the guard to speak to the owner of the farm. Their respectful response caught him off guard, and he went to look for Rúnarsson. A few moments later, Rúnarsson, who looked old but was still in great shape, stood in front of them, leaning proudly on his fence.

"What's brought you here? Where are you from?" Rúnarsson asked cautiously, but not in an unfriendly way.

"Good afternoon. We're from Romania and are traveling around Iceland because we want to raise Icelandic sheep in Romania, so we're visiting local farmers and talking to them about the work they do. We just couldn't go past your farm. Sorry if we're a nuisance or if we're distracting you from work," Danylo said. Rúnarsson took his bait.

"No, no, it's alright. We're always glad to have guests on this God-forsaken island. My name is Úlfur, I'm retired but I still fishing a bit, and I own this farm. It's just what I wanted to do when I got old. What are your names?" he asked. "Is there anything in particular you'd like to know?"

"My name is Adrian, and this is my friend Mircea. We're just curious about your vision and your experience with the farm – anything that has to do with sheep farming really," Danylo said. He was Adrian and

Bot was Mircea. Meanwhile, Sasha and Vincenzo quietly left them for a walk around the island.

"I have to say that these particular sheep have a difficult temperament. They often fight when they're in a flock together. The males can be aggressive because they're always struggling over leadership, and there's always the risk that one of them could seriously injure the other. You've got to be careful, a ram can sometimes decide that a human is dangerous and could attack them. As for their wool, our Icelandic sheep have long and thick coats, they're popular with producers of woolen clothing. The topcoat is usually rougher and is used for rugs, and the softer undercoat is used in the famous Icelandic knitwear. Their meat and milk are good to eat, too, and their skin can be used for making fine leather shoes. What can I say, they're excellent sheep all around," he said. "Why don't we get some beers at the local bar tonight, and you'll be able to try the mutton from my farm for yourselves? What do you think?"

"Gladly! We'd be delighted," Bot said.

"I fully agree. What time would be best for you?" Danylo asked.

"Let's say seven, but don't be late, as I can't stay for too long, I'm off for an overnight fishing trip later."

Danylo and his three friends arrived at the bar just before seven. Danylo and Bot got a quiet table in the corner; Sasha and his friend Vincenzo sat at the bar counter, pretending that they were there on holiday and didn't care in the slightest about sheep or anything to do with them. Rúnarsson arrived two minutes before seven with a bodyguard.

"Hello," he said, "I see you're right on time, good – young people these days have trouble with discipline. Meet my assistant Stephen," Danylo and Bot introduced themselves to Stephen and shook hands with him and Rúnarsson.

"Almost all of the lamb and mutton here is from my farm," Rúnarsson continued. "I can recommend the *hangikjöt*, a smoked lamb dish, it's my favorite dish here. I also love *svið*, charred sheep's head. Also, I don't know if they have it right now, but sometimes they serve *hrútspungar*, cured lamb testicles in aspic. And of course you must try the traditional lamb soup! I've not met anyone who didn't like it. And just to mention, we've caught all the fish on the menu here, but as far as I understand, you're here for meat feast tonight."

"Thank you. Both for coming to meet us and for this detailed account of traditional Icelandic dishes," Danylo replied. "Why don't we order four lamb soups, two charred heads, a double serving of smoked lamb, and four beers? Mircea and I are paying." Danylo wanted to get Rúnarsson on his side. Rúnarsson and Stephen nodded approvingly, and Danylo ordered with a server.

"Mr. Rúnarsson, what do you feed your sheep?" Bot asked.

"Well, we don't have a lot of space here on Flatey Island, so for the most part I buy hay and store it in the barn. On the main island, sheep spend the entire summer, up until October I would say, on pastures, then they are herded into pens and each farmer marks his sheep with a special tag. We only have about 300,000 people living in Iceland, but there are a million sheep, so sheep farming is quite common here. The sheep spend a lot of time grazing on the green hills swept by the sea breeze, and according to a popular belief, you don't even need to salt our lamb when you cook it."

After dinner and a beer, Rúnarsson left to prepare for his fishing trip. Stephen stayed behind with Danylo and Bot. In Rúnarsson's absence, he turned out to be much more sociable and friendly. Stephen, who was British, told them about his experience of working with and looking after sheep in Iceland. Sasha and Vincenzo joined them at the table and were listened carefully to Stephen, who was glad to be the center of attention. It was clear that he was a little bored with small island life and glad to talk to other people his age. Danylo ordered a liter of *Brennivín*, a local potato spirit, to keep the conversation going. Rúnarsson called Stephen around nine to tell him he was setting sail. Danylo and his squad were planning to get inside his house – and, if they could, the barn on his property – while he was away. The house was on the other side of the island, so they took the phone call as a signal that they could begin their operation. Bot asked Stephen if they could go look at Rúnarsson's sheep, and Stephen agreed, though reluctantly. Sasha, meanwhile, quickly headed to the cottage where they were staying to grab a bottle of whisky, to which he added a heavy dose of a sedative. He reunited with the rest of the men at Rúnarsson's farm, where they were all joined by Edward,

Rúnarsson's second bodyguard, who acted less warmly toward Danylo and his friends. Edward and Stephen stepped away from the rest of the men and spoke, each agitated, for a couple of minutes, but in the end joined the group again. Sasha poured everyone whisky, but while Edward and Stephen thirstily downed their shots, Danylo and the rest of them just pretended to and emptied their glasses whenever they could. An hour later, Stephen and Edward were deeply asleep on the sofa in the farm's outbuilding.

"Looks like they're out," Danylo said. "We can start."

"Fuck, guys, they won't die, will they?" Bot asked, worried.

Sasha said, "Relax, Bot, they'll be okay, look how big they are! I suggest splitting up. Vincenzo and I will check out what's happening at the barn, while you two have a look around the house. Yeah?" With the situation growing increasingly tense, Sasha took control.

"That's what we'll do. These two gorillas will sleep for another five or six hours, no doubt, but just to be safe, let's meet here again in an hour," Danylo replied, confident as ever. "Alright guys, let's do it."

Danylo and Bot entered the house without any issues. The doors stood open, which briefly worried them, but they kept their cool and began to look for whatever priceless thing might be hidden in the house. It was cozy inside. Antiques from every corner of the world were scattered throughout the house, but nothing that seemed out of the ordinary. Danylo walked up to the second floor while Bot stayed on the first. In the kitchen, Bot found a hidden door.

He called out to Danylo, "Hey, there's stairs to a basement here, come!"

Danylo ran down the stairs.

"Bot, you fucking loser, why the hell are you yelling?" he whispered, annoyed. "Come on, show me the basement."

"Sorry, sorry, that was stupid. Look, the stairway is here."

"Go on, let's see what's happening down there."

There were two rooms in the basement, a cellar and an office. They first looked around the cellar but didn't find anything other than a couple bottles of wine, a selection of top-quality whisky and rum, and a bunch of dry and canned goods. The office looked like a real haven, a peaceful corner and a source of inspiration. Countless figurines lined the wooden shelves above a radiator that stretched along one of the walls. The shelves along the opposite wall were filled with books. Antique sconces shaped like torches hung in the corners of the room. There was a rug with Arabic inscriptions and oriental patterns on the floor, and a pair of warm woolen slippers. The desk was by the wall farthest from the door, with a large, cushiony armchair – the kind you sink in and forget about the rest of the world – pulled up behind it. Danylo looked through the bookcase while Bot rummaged around in the drawers of the desk.

"There are some odd figurines here – I think they're made out of ivory – and a notebook filled with either runes or a code, I can't quite tell," Bot said to Danylo.

"And that's it? Fucking hell, this is a complete failure. Okay, let's get out of here and go look through the cottage where the bodyguards live."

Meanwhile, Sasha and Vincenzo quietly approached the barn and used a Swiss army knife to pry open the window and enter. The barn was divided into three parts. The main and largest part was a storage space for hay and farming equipment. There was also a walk-in fridge, and a small caretaker's room, equipped with a kitchenette. It was dark in the barn, so Sasha and Vincenzo turned on the flashlights on their phone. They looked through the caretaker's room first, then the fridge, and finally the storeroom, which was lined with bales of hay. They didn't find anything particularly interesting, except for a tractor trailer loaded with three bales of hay and a 50-liter black plastic barrel. Sasha jumped into the trailer, looked through the hay, and opened the barrel:

"Come here Vincenzo, I think we hit the jackpot."

Sasha and Vincenzo alternated between English and Italian when speaking to each other, but they understood each other very well. They'd spent lots of time working together and were good friends.

"Alright, let's see what you found," Vincenzo said, climbing up into the trailer. There were two dozen neat, brick-shaped packages tied together with Sellotape.

"Give me your knife, I'll cut this open and see what sort of stuff this is."

Sasha handed over the knife. "So what's your expert opinion?"

"*Fratello*, this is top-quality stuff, really amazing. Seems like this cocaine came straight from the producer," Vincenzo said, snorting and rubbing cocaine into his gums.

As Sasha and Vincenzo sampled the cocaine, a light outside was switched on, and an old man, eighty or so, walked into the barn. Sasha and Vincenzo laid down low on the bed of the trailer. Limping and muttering to himself in Icelandic, the old man headed to the kitchenette. He was short and had a thick white beard. The old man only stayed in the kitchen for about five minutes, then left, looking content, locked the barn door, and headed in an unknown direction.

"What do you think, Vincenzo?" Sasha turned to his friend. "Should we get Danylo and Bot and take this cocaine with us?"

"No, no, no, are you crazy? That's too dangerous, we'll get caught. Let's not rush. We need to think through this. At the very least, we need to have a boat or a ship at our disposal. The island is only a few dozen kilometers from the mainland. We'll get everything ready, come back, and take every last drop of it. We can kill this local Santa Klaus if we need to."

"You're right, you're right. No need to rush," Sasha said. "The most important thing is that we know where they keep the cocaine. Right, let's get out of here and tell the other two what we found. Danylo really knew what he was talking about!"

When Sasha and Vincenzo got back to Rúnarsson's house, Danylo and Bot were already waiting for them outside by the sheep pen. Danylo looked frustrated and irritated. Bot looked around nervously, visibly anxious to leave.

"What you got, any trophies?" Sasha asked enthusiastically. "Are the bodyguards still asleep?"

"Sound asleep. We've got nothing. We searched all over the house, but there's nothing. What about the barn?"

"I got good news! You were right, they must be using the barn as a shipment hub, Rúnarsson's got first-rate cocaine in there. At least a couple dozen kilos. He must get it straight from the producer, which means he's got some serious connections. Anyway, you were right, he's far from an ordinary, retired officer."

"Holy shit, what a twist. And here I was, thinking that we've gotten into all this for nothing. Alright, let's get back to the cottage and figure out what to do next."

They spent the rest of the night arguing over the best course of action but eventually decided that Vincenzo's plan made the most sense. In the morning, they all had breakfast together and went for a walk on the beach, mingling with other tourists. They then took the ferry back to Stykkishólmur. Meanwhile, Rúnarsson's two bodyguards, Stephen and Edward, woke up from their drug-induced sleep. They suspected that their drinks might have been spiked, but they weren't certain. Having made sure everything in Rúnarsson's house and in the barn was where it ought to be, they decided to conceal the incident from him. Stephen knew well that if their boss found out about the drinking at the farm, they would be in trouble. Rúnarsson was religious about order and discipline, and even the slightest deviation would have been reason enough for harsh punishment.

Danylo and his three friends arrived back in Reykjavík late that evening. Bot suggested they go for a walk in the city and get some beers. The rest of them gladly agreed. They settled down at Funny Bunny, an Irish pub perfect for the occasion.

"Thanks for coming guys," Danylo said to his friends. "Don't hold it against me that I tricked you into coming here. We'll still get to celebrate my bachelor's party and wedding. For now, let's drink to the four of us, to our courage and our luck. Cheers!" Everyone raised their glasses to Danylo's toast.

"Now back to business," Sasha took over. "Vincenzo and I will travel back to Rome early in the morning. We'll come up with a plan, find another two or three people to help out, and come back for another visit to Rúnarsson's farm in about two weeks. Danylo, your job is to hire a boat or small ship we could use. I don't think there'll be any issues with that. For our part, we'll bring someone who can sail and has the right paperwork for it."

"I agree, there's no point putting it off any longer. I'll handle the boat, don't worry about it."

"I'm going to stay here in Iceland for another two weeks then," Bot said. "No point going back and forth. I have my laptop with me, and there's access to WiFi."

At six on Monday morning, Danylo and Bot took Sasha and Vincenzo to the airport. Danylo still had another three days off, and he decided to spend them with Bot. They went to the port after dropping their friends at the airport to see what was available for hire and find out how much it would cost. Then they went back to the apartment on the outskirts of Reykjavík that Danylo had rented for his friends' visit. Danylo told Bot that using public transport made the most sense as far as getting around Reykjavík, both in terms of price and service. After the two had lunch, Danylo took a nap, while Bot set up in front of his laptop. Danylo slept for an hour and a half before he was woken up by Bot.

"Danylo, get up – you have to get up right now!" Bot yelled.

"Fucking hell, what's wrong with you? What happened? I was sleeping so well," Danylo got up and walked over to where Bot was sitting.

"I don't really know where to begin…"

"Look Bot, cut the shit. What's going on?"

"I'll tell you, I'll tell you, but you really should sit down first," Bot said. "Do you remember, when we were in Rúnarsson's office, I found a notebook in his desk drawer? It was a Moleskine notebook – I have a similar one, but Rúnarsson's seems like a luxury edition or something."

"I remember you said it had some weird script in it."

"Well, I took it. I mean, I stole it. Just shoved it under my clothes without any of you noticing. But what I've since realized is that it's not just some random hieroglyphics inside, but a text written in Nüshu, a Chinese script, and Caesar cipher. I scanned a couple of pages yesterday and sent them to my friend Xiaolong via the darknet. Xiaolong is an amazing programmer from Guangzhou, he's obsessed with all sorts of encryption and cryptography. He just sent me the text he decrypted. I'm a bit shocked. Rúnarsson's been using the notebook for years to keep track of cocaine shipments to ports across Europe, the names of border guards and police officers who were bribed, the names of people who've ordered murders and assassinations, the names of members of the European Parliament and the UK House of Commons financed by criminal syndicates and Russian special services, bank account details. He's noted the year, month, and date, and sometimes even the exact hour when each of the things in this notebook happened.

"Holy fuck, Bot, what have you done?" Danylo yelled. "Do you understand how fucked we are? We have to get out of here as soon as we can, because Rúnarsson's going to realize real quick that his precious Moleskine is gone. Maybe he already has! Maybe he's also realized we're the ones to blame, and he's already searching for us! We got get our shit together and get the hell out of here. A good friend of mine, Alvydas, from Lithuania, is a manager at a logistics firm, he has contacts in the port and can probably help us get to Europe on a cargo ship. It's better if we stay away from the airport."

***

Late on Monday morning, Rúnarsson – who was in a particularly good mood that day – walked into his office, settled into the chair behind his desk, and stretched his arms over his head, yawning. As he opened his desk drawer, his mood turned to dust. His notebook was missing. He had a rule: always leave the Moleskine in the same place. Knowing he wouldn't have put it anywhere else, still he frantically threw open the other drawers, but the notebook was nowhere to be found.

Rúnarsson ran out of his office and yelled for Stephen, "Where the hell are you?"

"I'm here Mr. Rúnarsson!" Stephen called from beside the outbuilding.

Rúnarsson, all fury and no words, walked up to him and punched him in the face. Stephen fell to the ground.

"You bastard! Who's been in my office while I was fishing?"

Stephen got up, frightened, and pressed his hands to his face.

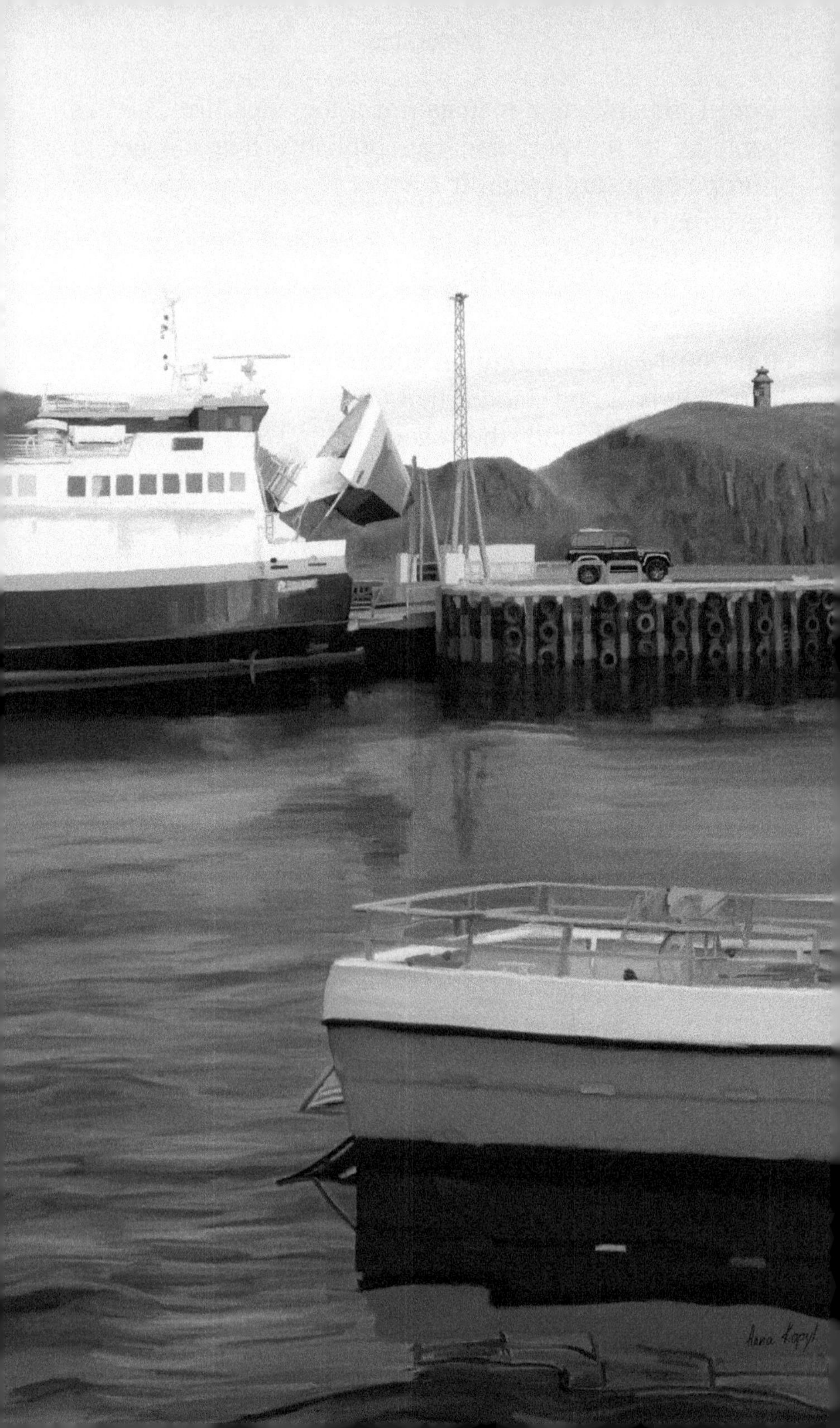

"I swear, Mr. Rúnarsson, Edward and I would never enter your office without your permission," Stephen got up, frightened and pressing his hands to his face.

"Who could it have been, then? Can you tell me? Or do you two want to make a fool out of me?"

"No, never. When… when you went fishing, those Romanians came over to have a look at the sheep farm."

"And?" Rúnarsson yelled.

"They brought whisky with them, we all drank, and we must've had too much. Edward and I blacked out, neither of us remembers much," Stephen said.

"Are the goods still there? Have you checked?"

"Yes, I checked as soon as I came to, everything's alright."

"You fucking idiots, do you know totally they fucked you over? They broke into my house while you were out. Your stupid head can't fathom the problems we're going to have now. Tell the men to get the ship ready immediately, we're leaving for to Stykkishólmur."

***

Wasting no time, Danylo called Sasha, explained what had happened, and asked him to either come meet them in the port of Kiel, in Germany, with a car, or get someone he trusted to do so. Kiel was one of the closest mainland ports to Scandinavia. Danylo and Bot then went straight to the offices of Danylo's friend's logistics firm. Alvydas wasn't there, and they waited for over two hours. While they waited, they fabricated a story that would prompt Alvydas to help them. They would tell him a couple of Danylo's friends came to stay with him over the weekend, and when they were all out on Friday night, they got into a fight with another group of men, and while Danylo and his friends fled the scene, the other guys called the police and filed a complaint, because two of them ended up in the hospital. The idea was to ask Alvydas to use his contacts in the port to help him and Bot leave the island to avoid criminal liability. They would of course also offer generous remuneration for his help. When Alvydas finally arrived, and the two told their story, Alvydas took a few minutes to mull it over, then left the office and told Danylo and Bot to wait for him there. He promised to do everything he could to get them out of the mess they were in. Danylo and Bot relaxed a bit, feeling more confident. While Alvydas was out, Danylo's phone rang. Oleh Velychko's name popped up on the screen, Borys's nephew.

"Hi Danylo," Oleh said. "Have you seen my uncle or Magnus by any chance? They've both disappeared and neither of them is picking up their phone."

"Hey, no, I haven't heard from them. Why are you worried?" Danylo asked, "Did something happen?"

"No, I think everything's okay, but it's nine now, and I haven't heard anything from them. Uncle Borys is usually back from work by six."

"Don't worry Oleh, he must be held up at one of the sites, or maybe he's getting dinner out," Danylo said, feeling that something was off. He decided that reassuring Oleh would be better than scaring him more.

"Okay, see you soon then, have a nice evening," said Oleh.

"You too. Let me know if you hear anything." Danylo hung up.

Danylo turned to Bot as soon as he hung up.

"I'm not totally sure, but my gut feeling is that we've been busted."

"We have no choice but to wait for Alvydas. At least we're safe here," Bot replied.

***

Rúnarsson and his two bodyguards were at Hjörtur Skúlason's house in Garðabær in no time. Rúnarsson stormed into Skúlason's office and slammed the door shut behind himself.

"Hjörtur, listen carefully to me. Something very valuable went missing from my house on Flatey Island last night. I have strong suspicions about who did it. There was a group of men who said they were tourists from Romania and wanted to learn more about my sheep farm. Get all our guys together at your work office and call Mariusz – we could use a couple of his Poles – they know all the gossip around here. Here's a USB drive with a video from the bar where I had dinner with them before heading out for an overnight fishing trip. Show it to everyone, maybe someone will recognize them. And remember," he spoke slowly and deliberately, "if we can't find them, we're both dead. Got it?"

"Yes," Skúlason said, taking the USB drive. "Let me just have a look at the video while you're here."

"Be quick, every minute counts."

Skúlason stared at his computer screen, then flinched and froze.

"Well, Hjörtur," Rúnarsson demanded, "do you recognize anyone?"

"Yes, I know this guy in the hat. He works with the construction team at my neighbor's house."

Now it was Skúlason's turn to speak slowly.

"It all makes sense now… Someone recently broke into my house while I was away camping with my family and stole seventy thousand bucks. I couldn't report it to the police and was too embarrassed to tell anyone else."

"You fool," shouted Rúnarsson, "you should've told me! That must be how they figured out about me. Call your neighbor and find out where this fucking asshole from the construction site is."

"I can, but I have a better idea. I can call the owner of the construction firm that's in charge of the works there. My wife has been thinking about renovating our summer house, so I have his number."

"Well, I guess we can't do anything while we're here on your street, there are too many witnesses here. Get him to come out to your firm's storage depot. Tell him you have an urgent order you need to discuss with him. I'll get him talking once he gets there. Stop staring at me and call him, now!"

"Just a second, I'm trying to remember how I entered his name into my contacts."

***

Alvydas got back to his office just after 9pm. He had good news for Danylo and Bot: his friend, captain of a Danish cargo ship, said he would take them to Aarhus, one of Denmark's largest ports. The ship would leave Reykjavík at 11:45pm. Danylo called Sasha and told him he and Bot would be in Aarhus three days later. Alvydas drove them to the port. Each sat in his own silence on the way there, each consumed by his own thoughts and worries. Bot was more anxious than the other two: he knew he would be very seasick but decided not to tell Danylo. He had no other choice but to get on the ship, so he had to accept his lot, so cruelly dealt to him by the whimsical Lady Fortuna. Just after 11pm, Danylo and Bot found themselves in the warm and cozy captain's cabin onboard the ship, awaiting their long journey across the cold and mysterious Atlantic. Danylo's phone rang, first with several calls from Borys, then from his boss Magnus. He didn't pick up. When it kept ringing, he walked out onto the deck and threw his phone into the ocean.

***

Skúlason, Rúnarsson, and the two bodyguards drove from Skúlason's house to Kópavogur and called Danylo's boss Magnus using a new, British SIM-card. Skúlason asked Magnus if they could meet promptly as he had an urgent and important order. They agreed to meet at 9pm outside Skúlason's firm's storage depot. Magnus was out with Borys shopping for building materials; they went to the meeting together. The depot was in the middle of nowhere, in a deserted neighborhood just outside Reykjavík. It was getting dark, the wind was howling, and the drizzle that had started that morning turned into rain. Skúlason greeted Magnus and Borys and took him to a small office inside the depot.

When Borys saw Skúlason his heart sank, but he held himself together and buried his nervousness.

"Glad to see you, Magnus," Skúlason began. "I've heard good things about your firm, so I decided to turn to you with an important request. An urgent request. I'm just waiting on my partner, who should be here any moment now, before we get down to the business of it. And who's this with you? I feel like I've seen him working on my neighbor's house. Would either of you like some tea or coffee? The weather's bleak today," he said slyly.

"I'm glad you've heard good things about the firm," said Magnus. "Good feedback always drives me to grow and improve. This here is Borys, he manages the construction workers I employ. He's my foreman. And no tea or coffee, thank you – just had some hotdogs and coffee on our way here. Could you just give me a quick idea of what sort of thing you're looking for?"

"You see, it's quite a delicate matter," Skúlason said. He saw headlights flash in the window and heard a car approach. "That must be my partner. I think he'll be better able to explain what this is all about."

As Skúlason spoke, Rúnarsson and his two bodyguards walked into the room.

"Alright, Magnus Gunnarsson, let's talk. Stephen, Edward, take these two to the depot and make sure they're comfortable."

Stephen and Edward complied, dragging Borys and Magnus into the open space of the depot. When Rúnarsson stepped out of the office, the two were tied to the chairs they were sitting on. Magnus was frightened and looked around blearily without comprehending what was going on. Borys stared at the floor in front of him and his chest rose and fell as he beathed. Rúnarsson grabbed a stool and pulled it up close to them.

"Magnus," he said, "I think you understand that the circumstances are rather serious, so I recommend that you're as honest as possible. A valuable object has recently gone missing from my house. I have grounds to believe it was stolen by someone who works for you. Hjörtur, give me the laptop," Rúnarsson said, then played the video from the Flatey Island bar, which showed Danylo and Bot. "Do you know either of these men?" Rúnarsson asked.

"Yes, I know one of them. His name is Danylo, he works at my firm," answered Magnus.

"When is the last time you saw him or talked to him?"

"Last week. He took a couple of days off. He said his family was coming over to Iceland and he wanted to show them around."

"Did he say where they were going to go? Do you know any of his relatives who came over?"

"He didn't say where exactly, just mentioned the Golden Circle and Húsavík. And I have no idea who was visiting him, I've never met any of his family members," Magnus said and changed the topic, "Please help Borys! He seems really unwell."

"Listen to me carefully," Rúnarsson said, his face almost touching Magnus's. "Shut your fucking mouth and do what you're told. For now, just shut the fuck up. Stephen, take Borys's phone and untie his hands. Make him call Danylo, then pass the phone to me."

"Call Danylo," Stephen yelled at Borys, waving the phone in front of his face.

Borys did what he was told. Stephen gave the phone to Rúnarsson. He rang Danylo's number three times, but there was no answer. Rúnarsson lost his temper and punched Borys in the face. Borys fell off his chair into a heap on the floor.

"Now give me Magnus's phone," Rúnarsson instructed his bodyguards, "and tie Borys back to his chair." He made another two attempts to call Danylo, this time from Magnus's phone.

Borys didn't make a sound, but his breathing grew heavier and more obstructed.

"I swear I have nothing to do with Danylo and whatever he and his friends did!" Magnus said. "I'm begging you, at least give Borys some water!"

"Hjörtur, go get a glass of water from the office."

Skúlason immediately obeyed.

"Now Stephen, give this guy some water."

"Boss, I don't think he's breathing," Stephen said.

"Check his pulse!"

"There's no pulse, Mr. Rúnarsson."

"Fuck, that's just what we needed, a dead body. Stephen, Edward, put him into the trunk," Rúnarsson said, then turned around, pulled out a gun, and shot Magnus in the forehead. "Take this one, too."

Part 3.

Roman holiday

Danylo and Bot's trip to Aarhus was uneasy. Bot was relentlessly sick. Once in Aarhus, the pair boarded a bus to Flensburg, Germany's northernmost town, where Sasha met them in his car. They headed to Rome. It was a long journey across most of Europe, nearly 2,000 kilometers. All three were nervous and none wanted to bring up the circumstances that had led to their meeting. After a few hours on the road, they stopped at a gas station for a snack and to use the restroom, and they felt the tension ease as their bodies finally began to adjust to the new reality. Sasha was first to break the silence.

"So what now? This is a complete fucking mess. Do you even realize who we're dealing with? Because I can't make sense of any of it. It's like a fucking spy movie."

"There's one thing I can tell you for sure, brother," Danylo said, "We have to take all this shit more than seriously, even if at first glance it might seem like a delirious dream." He looked exhausted but serious and determined.

"Alright, fine. So what do you suggest? Do you have a plan?" asked Sasha. "Because we already nearly failed in Kyiv once and I don't want any of that mess again. Look, I've got a family. My life's just about gone back to normal."

"First let's get to Rome. We'll lay low once we get there and try to figure out what's happening in Iceland. Then we'll act in accordance with the situation. At least that's how I see it," Danylo said. "Have you spoken to Vincenzo?"

Sasha shook his head.

"Doesn't sound like a great plan to me. Yes, I briefly spoke to Vincenzo, but didn't give him the details. I told him we'll get together when I'm back in Rome to discuss what comes next. I hardly know what's happening myself, and as far I can tell, neither do you. Good thing you had the sense to get the fuck out of Iceland. But tell me, Bot," he said, turning to face him, "why on earth did you grab that notebook?"

"I really don't know, I can't explain, it just happened. I'm so sorry for fucking up." Bot stared into space, barely alive and clinging to the back seat of the car.

"Don't kick yourself, Bot," Danylo turned to his friend. "It's all my fault, really. I got you all to come to Reykjavík and into this mess."

"Good thing you can admit to your own fuck-up," Sasha said with bitter irony.

As soon as they got to Rome they called Vincenzo, who texted Sasha the address of a flat where they could stay. The flat was in the central Pigna neighborhood, not far from the Pantheon. The neighborhood's streets bustled with tourists, so it was easy for Danylo, Bot, and Sasha to blend in with the crowd and not attract too much attention. Vincenzo's family, the Farinellas, owned restaurants and night clubs all over Italy. They'd purchased the flat for the countless family members and friends who came to visit them in Rome.

Vincenzo had been brought up to mistrust strangers, but he was always generous and fair with his friends. His father, Giuseppe Farinella, came from Sicily, but was a respected and influential figure in Rome. Young Giuseppe came to Rome to study and stayed there afterwards. His father and uncle had just opened their first two restaurants there and he was left in charge of their management. Cosimo, Giuseppe's father and Vincenzo's grandfather – a man of honor and the head of one of the clans that ruled Palermo – and Cosimo's brother Paolo founded a restaurant business that grew every year. By the time Danylo and Bot arrived in Rome, the Farinella family owned twenty-four restaurants and eleven clubs. The Farinellas' success was made possible by Cosimo's foresight: he organized his son's marriage to Francesca Montolivo, thus forming an alliance between Sicilians and Calabrians, representatives of the Ndrangheta, the largest mafia association in Italy. Vincenzo spent his childhood between Sicily and Calabria. He was brought up under strict discipline, in accordance with the mafia's traditions. From a young age, he was taught that money must be accumulated, not squandered. Of course, Vincenzo loved luxury cars and beautiful women, but he always remained prudent and pragmatic. He lived with his family in a lavish mansion in the Balduina neighborhood.

Sasha drove to the apartment, where they were greeted by a maid who gave them the keys and left. The flat was on the fourth floor; it had two bedrooms, a living room, a kitchen, two bathrooms, and a large balcony overlooking the city – a luxury apartment in the heart of the Eternal City. Vincenzo wasn't there yet. He had a few business meetings to attend to first, but rushed to meet Danylo, Bot, and Sasha as soon as he was free. He could feel the eye of the storm approaching and loved the adrenaline that came with this feeling. He rang the apartment's bell just as the three men were finishing the sandwiches they'd quickly put together with whatever they could find in the kitchen.

"*Ciao, ragazzi!*" Vincenzo burst into the apartment. "How was the journey? I hope you are comfortable here. You hungry? I can order us something. One of our restaurants is just around the corner."

"The journey was fine, thank God," Sasha replied. "Don't worry about food, we're just finishing some sandwiches, but thanks for the offer."

"*Va bene.* Then tell me what's happened, I can tell from looking at you that you're in trouble. Can you explain to me what's going on, Danylo?"

Danylo explained, in detail, everything that had happened since they'd parted ways, and why he and Bot were suddenly forced to flee Iceland. Vincenzo listened carefully, then looked each of them in the eye, from one to the next.

"*Mai dai, cazzo,*" he said, finally. "So you have this notebook with you?"

"Yes, right here. I'll show you." Danylo pulled the Moleskine from his bag and handed it over to Vincenzo.

"It's almost full. Only a few empty pages left. Very much information. All of you, and me also, will get killed! No, not just killed – butchered and fed to pigs," said Vincenzo. "Okay, we must start acting right now, we have no time to waste. I'm will go and get a man I trust who can help to understand this. Wait for me here."

"Wait, Vincenzo, why don't we get a new SIM-card? We can go away from the flat and call my friends back in Iceland to figure out what's going on there. Otherwise we'll be useless just sitting here," Danylo suggested. As always, he was calm and confident.

"Okay, good idea. Stay in touch."

Sasha took Danylo and Bot to the Piazza Mastai in Trastevere, a neighborhood of bars and clubs equally beloved by Roman youth and by tourists, looking for fun and cocktails. Once at the square, the three sat on a bench near a beautiful fountain that was commissioned by Pope Pius IX in the 19th century. They decided to first call Alvydas to find out whether he'd heard anything.

"Hi Alvydas, how are you?" Danylo said. "It's me, Danylo, just wanted to say thank you for your help."

"Hello Danylo. I've tried calling you so many times, but you must've gotten rid of your old phone. Do you have any idea what's going on over here?"

"No, what?" Danylo asked anxiously.

"Your boss, Magnus, is missing. He was last seen on the day you and your friend boarded that ship. I don't know – and I don't want to know – what happened, but don't ever call me again," Alvydas said and hung up.

Danylo was quiet for a moment. He stared blankly at the fountain in front of him. Bot couldn't bear the silence.

"What happened?" asked Bot.

"I think it's a total fucking mess," Danylo answered, unable to break his stare.

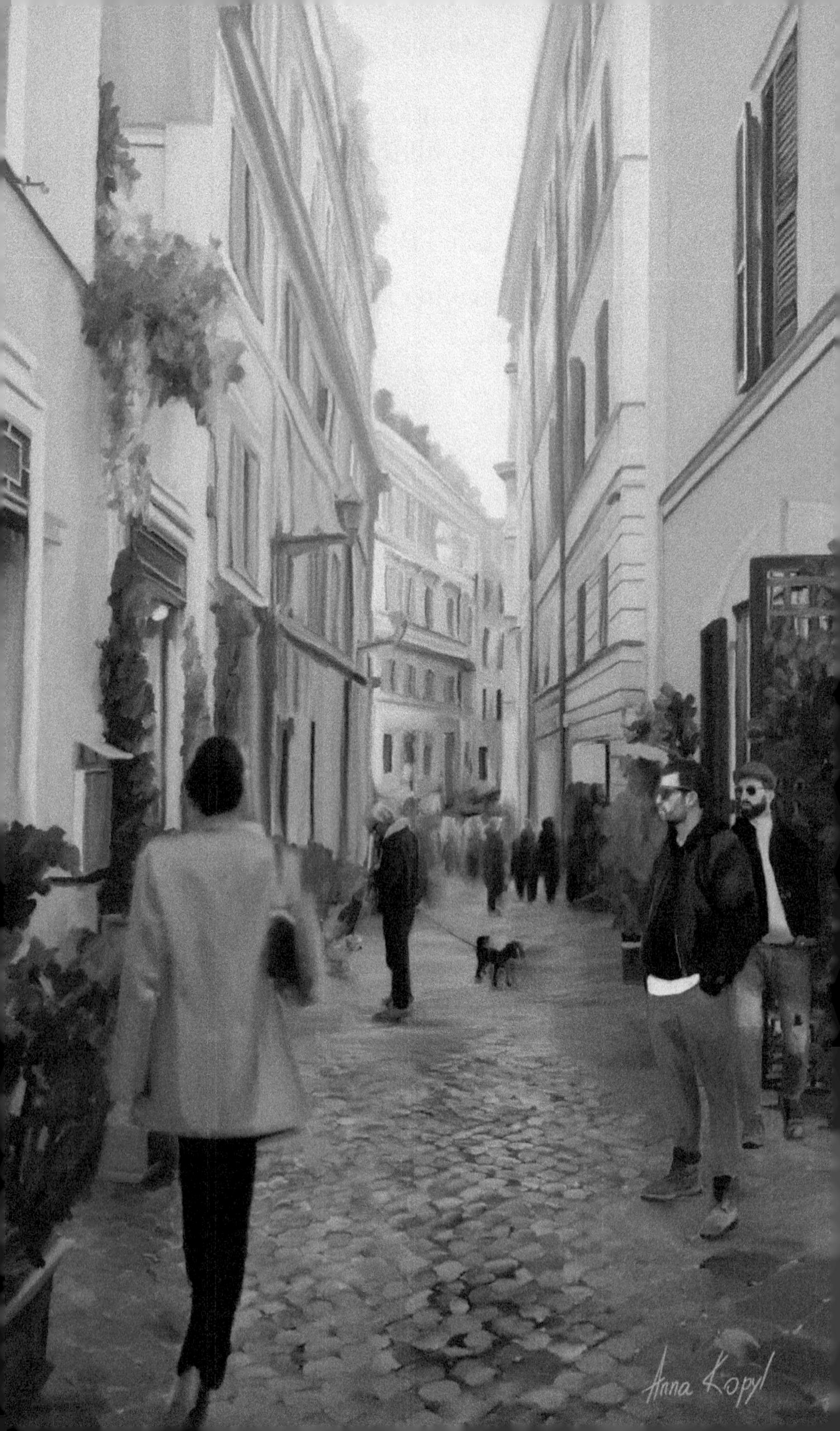
Anna Kopyl

Moleskine

They went back to the flat. Bot searched Icelandic news websites for information. Magnus Gunnarson was indeed missing and was being searched for by the police. Now the group realized how close they were to being caught. They hadn't expected one call to change their perspective so definitively, but Magnus's disappearance had set a whole chain of events in motion. They were now fighting for survival. Sasha called Vincenzo and asked him to return to the flat as soon as possible. Vincenzo arrived within an hour, with two armed men he asked to stand watch outside the door. He had by now fully grasped the seriousness of the situation and gave Danylo and his friends two guns.

"Sasha, Danylo here you are," he said, handing them the guns. "Hopefully they make you feel more at ease. I will be glad if you don't have to use them, but keep them with you for now. You called a friend in Iceland, right? What is the news there?"

Danylo and Sasha exchanged a glance.

Sasha said, "Bad news. Danylo's boss, Magnus, has gone missing. The police are searching for him."

"Woah, that was fast. But maybe the notebook is not the reason behind his disappearance? Maybe he had other dealings you did not know about, and the timing is just a coincidence? What do you think?" asked Vincenzo.

"I'm a hundred per cent sure that his disappearance is to do with the notebook," Danylo said. "My boss is an honest man and definitely was not involved in any criminal stuff. Of course as a businessman, he sometimes tried to swipe the state or his competitors, but he always knew where to draw the line. He always paid us on time and treated his workers with respect and compassion. In all the time that I worked for him, he never wronged any of his workers or really anyone else he knew. And to be honest, I feel guilty now. He may have suffered because of my stupidity."

"Don't beat yourself up before we really know what happened," Bot tried to reassure his friend. "You don't know for sure why he disappeared, and you're also not the only one to blame in this situation. Now is not the time to lose heart, we got get out of this mess, and we can only do it with cool heads."

"*Va bene*," Vincenzo took the initiative in his hands. "I think we must contact the Moleksine's owner and define the rules of the game, because if they get to us first, we are fucked. Professor Federico Castellazzi is coming to Rome tomorrow, he will help to decrypt the text in the notebook. And don't worry, he is a family friend and can be trusted."

"I'll try to find the number of the hotel on Flatey Island online, maybe they can help us get in touch with Rúnarsson," Bot said.

"Ah, great idea, Bot," said Sasha.

"I agree," Vincenzo nodded.

The next day, Vincenzo met Professor Castellazzi as he alighted from his early morning train and drove him to the apartment. The professor began work on the notebook immediately, and Bot helped. Bot found the number of the hotel on Flatey Island, and Danylo, Sasha, and Vincenzo embarked on negotiations with Rúnarsson. Danylo called the hotel and asked the receptionist to tell Mr. Rúnarsson that a friend of his from Romania was urgently trying to get in touch and would call back in two hours. Danylo immediately got rid of both the phone and the SIM-card he used to make the call and moved to another location. Vincenzo drove Danylo and Sasha far away from the crowds, to an Ostia beach. Exactly two hours after his first call, Danylo called the hotel again. The receptionist told him that Mr. Rúnarsson was on a work trip but left a phone number Danylo could use to get in touch with him. Danylo thanked the receptionist and hung up, then gathered himself and dialled the number he was given.

"Hello, Mr. Rúnarsson, this is –"

Rúnarsson cut him off.

"I know who you are, Danylo. I was expecting a call from you. Were you not told as a child that you can't take other people's things? You could pay dearly for something like this. You're so young, what are you ruining your life for?"

"Listen," said Danylo, "I'll give you your notebook back, just let Magnus go and don't touch anyone else."

"Magnus who? I don't know anyone called Magnus," Rúnarsson said coolly. "It hadn't even crossed my mind to harm anyone. I hope you've had sense enough to keep your mouth shut about the notebook, because otherwise I won't be quite so friendly. Your sister is such a beauty – I think she'll be a good doctor."

Silence.

"Okay, Danylo."

Danylo's breath broke across the line.

"When and where will I get my notebook back?"

"Rome, Italy. Tomorrow at 9pm. I'll send the exact coordinates tomorrow."

"Rome. Italy."

The words seemed to leak from Rúnarsson's mouth.

"Be sensible and remember, everything's in your hands. Bye bye."

The line went dead.

Danylo stuck out two fingers toward Vincenzo, meaning cigarette, got out of the car, and leaned on the hood. A small apparition of orange at the end of the fag. The other men, too, got out of the car.

"What did he say?" Sasha asked.

"He knows everything about me and my family." Danylo said. "Can I use your phone, Sasha?"

Danylo dialled his sister Veronika's number.

"Hey," he spoke around his cigarette, into the receiver, "how are you?"

"Danylo, is that you? Where are you? How are you doing?" asked Veronika. "We haven't heard from you in a while, and you haven't been answering our messages either. Mom's really worried!"

"Listen to me, Veronika, and please don't interrupt me. I'm fine – I'm alive and well. But you, mom, and Mykhailo have to leave Ivano-Frankivsk right now, for at least a week. I'm not joking," Danylo said, eyes closed and rubbing his forehead. "Please, just do what I say."

"What happened Danylo?" Veronika asked.

Silence.

"What did you do!"

"I'm sorry, I can't," said Danylo flatly. "Just trust me. Take mom and our brother and get as far away from home as you can. Don't tell anyone where you're going, just disappear for a while. I have to go now, but promise you'll do what I said."

For a moment Veronika said nothing.

"I don't know what the fuck is going on, but please be careful. I promise. Whatever. Please."

***

Rúnarsson knew full well that he was no longer in control. His comfortable retirement had been plunged into the dark of chaos. Having always been the pursuer, he was now forced into the terminal crouch of prey. A military man, but somehow unprepared for this. Oh Lady Fortuna, she does what she pleases. After the disappearance of the notebook, Rúnarsson had no choice but to let its true owner – the shadow who entrusted him with the information – Sir Raymond Miles, in on the catastrophe. The theft had undone all of

Rúnarsson's past achievements and accomplishments, and he was forced to come grovelling to his boss, humiliated like a dog. Sir Raymond, in his medieval estate in County Merseyside near Liverpool; from English aristocracy, royal family retainer; incredibly powerful and unthinkably rich, with business interests the world over. Sir Raymond and Rúnarsson's friendship several decades old – dating to when Sir Raymond was the UK ambassador to Colombia and then Peru, and Rúnarsson was in charge of the diplomatic mission's security. After that, Rúnarsson travelled the former British colonies on secret military missions. How many he'd carried out he didn't know, different missions serving in different military units, but always remaining loyal to Sir Raymond, who had a small private army of his own to protect the oil fields and precious stone and metal deposits. His little military had other purposes, mopping-up British special services operations, sabotage and kidnapping and killing. Sir Raymond bought up land in Peru. Registered it with front men. Besides coffee, he also grew the coca plant. The plantations were guarded by only the cream of private army's crop. Sir Raymond – ever distrustful of digital information records – once again enlisted Rúnarsson to help him devise a system. Every month, a parcel from Sir Raymond would arrive for Rúnarsson, wherever he happened to be. Among other things, the parcel always contained a tin of Peruvian coffee. In the slim space between the two walls of the double-insulated tin, Sir Raymond slid a sheet of paper scribed with the most up-to-date information about his transactions and dealings. He then popped a lid on it,

Moleskine

sealed it, and shipped it off to Rúnarsson. Rúnarsson, in turn, transcribed all the information into the Moleskine – a unique and singular database that had no copies or back-ups. It was, in other words, invaluable.

Rúnarsson walked into Sir Raymond's office with his teeth clenched but his head held high.

"Good afternoon, Sir Raymond. Glad to see you again, though unfortunately I come bearing bad news."

Raymond looked at him from his chair.

"Good afternoon Mr. Rúnarsson. I have, in fact, heard something about the difficulty you've run into. You know that I have eyes and ears everywhere, and especially in places where I have business interests. But I must admit – I couldn't believe it. Please explain how it is possible that the notebook went missing, and how such an experienced man could be so negligent?"

"I have no excuse, and the blame for this failure lies entirely with me. But I would venture to guess that the special services of a foreign state must be behind this. However, the people who undertook it are hired hands, puppets. Mutual friends of ours gave me information on their leader. Tonight, I'm flying to Rome with a group of trained men. Tomorrow we will have the Moleskine back."

"My dear friend, MI6 has already given me a rather comprehensive account of who, exactly, it was that tricked you. And I have to disappoint you. They weren't professionals at all. Just a group of ordinary men. Or perhaps we shouldn't say ordinary, given that they were able to pull this off. But enough talk, Mr. Rúnarsson. What happened, happened. And the fact of the matter is that you have lost something that I entrusted you with. You have one last chance to rectify the situation. I want the Moleskine on my desk the day after tomorrow, and I want everyone involved in its theft punished. Am I clear?"

"Yes sir. I'll get it done."

***

Vincenzo and Sasha convinced Danylo to go along with their plan. In reality, he had no other choice. Vincenzo believed that as long as they had the Moleskine, they had leverage over Rúnarsson and his people. They were untouchable. Sasha agreed. But as soon as Rúnarsson had the Moleskine back in his possession, they'd be killed. Vincenzo's idea was to give Rúnarsson a copy of the notebook and lure him into a trap. Vincenzo had the backing of Rome's criminal underworld, and Sasha, Danylo, and Bot came around to the plan. Danylo wasn't thrilled but knew there was no going back – putting all their cards on the table wasn't the worst option. Bot and Professor Castellazzi worked relentlessly on decrypting the notebook. Vincenzo couldn't get the image of his family ascending to the top echelon of the European elite out of his head, because of him, because of his plan. He was obsessed with this idea, though he didn't mention it to the others. Danylo had a hunch about what was driving Vincenzo, but on the other hand, he felt out of touch with reality. He was exhausted and lost and felt that all he could do was stick it out until the bitter end.

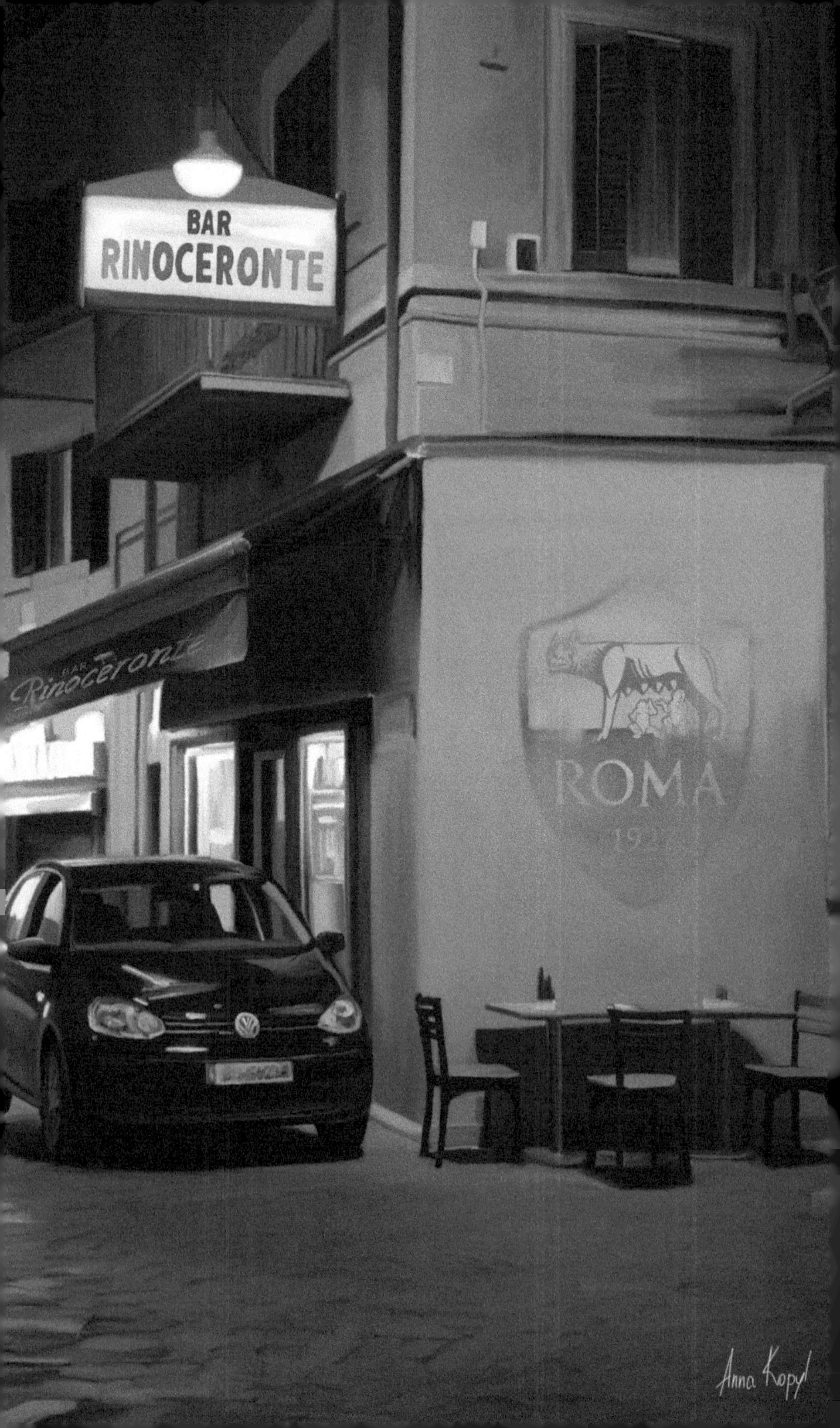
BAR
RINOCERONTE
BAR
Rinoceronte
ROMA
Anna Kopyl

One of Vincenzo's friends and business partners, Salvatore "Machete", controlled one of the most dangerous areas of Rome, San Basilio. The residential neighborhood sat in the northwest of the city, far from the center. It was here that Vincenzo planned to arrange the meeting with Rúnarsson. He asked Machete for help.

Machete agreed, sending ten of his people. The meeting with Rúnarsson was set to take place in the Rinoceronte bar on Via Corinaldo. A man in a green hat would enter the bar at 9pm and give Rúnarsson or whoever was representing him a bag containing a copy of the Moleskine. The man would then quickly leave. Meanwhile, Machete's men would capture Rúnarsson or his accomplices – or better still, both – shove them into a minibus parked nearby, and drive them to Vincenzo's country villa, where they would be locked in a basement. Sasha wanted to get personally involved in the operation. Danylo and Bot tried to talk him out of it, but he wouldn't listen.

Danylo texted Rúnarsson the name and location of the bar and a description of the man who would hand him the notebook. Machete's men kept an eye on the area. Danylo, Sasha, and Vincenzo arrived at Via Corinaldo just after 8pm and parked their Mercedes Benz CLS near Rinoceronte. Sasha walked over to talk to Cesare, the leader of Machete's men. The other two stayed in the car. Sasha was eager to curry favor with Vincenzo: he had his sights on working for the family, and had decided that now was the time to show how useful and capable he could be. Cesare's people took up positions all around Rinoceronte. Three men in a minibus parked next to the bar; two inside the bar; two smoked and talked loudly outside, by the entrance; another worked in the bar's kitchen; another two unloaded deliveries by the back door, in the passage to the courtyard of the residential building where the bar was situated.Sasha and Cesare sat in a car across from the bar, closely monitoring everything on the street. Two minutes before nine, a Volkswagen Touareg pulled up out front. Rúnarsson and another man, stocky and wearing a long coat, got out of the car. The driver got out after them, looked around, and stood next to the car's trunk. Rúnarsson and the man in the coat entered the bar. The young man in the green hat, the courier who would deliver the notebook to Rúnarsson, walked in behind them. He handed the bag with the notebook to Rúnarsson and turned to leave the bar. He didn't. Rúnarsson lifted a pistol and shot him twice, in the heart and in the head. Machete's men reached for their guns, but the man in the coat was faster. From his coat came a Belgian FN P90 submachine gun and he shot all four that were in the bar. The three men in the minibus ran out toward the bar, but a sniper on the roof of a nearby building downed two of them. Rúnarsson shot the third.

As Sasha and Cesare opened their doors, a bullet hit Sasha in the chest. He fell to the ground, unconscious. Rúnarsson's driver walked from where he had stood against the front door to the trunk, lifted out a hand-held anti-tank grenade launcher and fired at the bar. Tires screeched and three men on Ducati Panigales tore around the corner. Rúnarsson and his men, whisked off into the night like Joker in the sleepy Gotham, were gone.

---

*Available worldwide from Amazon
and all good bookstores*

Michael Terence Publishing

www.mtp.agency

mtp.agency

@mtp_agency